P9-EMH-588

DISCARD

BOB HONEY

WHO JUST DO STUFF

BOB HONEY

WHO JUST DO STUFF

A Novel

SEAN PENN

ATRIA BOOKS

New York   London   Toronto   Sydney   New Delhi

ATRIA
BOOKS

An Imprint of Simon & Schuster, Inc.
1230 Avenue of the Americas
New York, NY 10020

This book is a work of fiction. Any references to historical events, real people, or real places are used fictitiously. Other names, characters, places, and events are products of the author's imagination, and any resemblance to actual events or places or persons, living or dead, is entirely coincidental.

Copyright © 2016, 2018 by Clyde Is Hungry Films, Inc.

Page 163, Credits and Permissions, constitutes an extension of the copyright page.

All rights reserved, including the right to reproduce this book or portions thereof in any form whatsoever. For information, address Atria Books Subsidiary Rights Department, 1230 Avenue of the Americas, New York, NY 10020.

First Atria Books hardcover edition March 2018
Portions of this material were previously published in audio format under the same title in 2016.

ATRIA BOOKS and colophon are trademarks of Simon & Schuster, Inc.

For information about special discounts for bulk purchases, please contact Simon & Schuster Special Sales at 1-866-506-1949 or business@simonandschuster.com.

The Simon & Schuster Speakers Bureau can bring authors to your live event. For more information, or to book an event, contact the Simon & Schuster Speakers Bureau at 1-866-248-3049 or visit our website at www.simonspeakers.com.

Interior design by Amy Trombat

Manufactured in the United States of America

10 9 8 7 6 5 4

Library of Congress Cataloging-in-Publication Data
Names: Penn, Sean, 1960– author.
Title: Bob Honey who just do stuff : a novel / Sean Penn.
Description: New York : Atria Books, 2018.
Identifiers: LCCN 2017060020 (print) | LCCN 2018002029 (ebook) |
    ISBN 9781501189067 (ebook) | ISBN 9781501189043 (hardback)
Subjects: | BISAC: FICTION / Literary. | FICTION / Satire.
Classification: LCC PS3616.E5555 (ebook) | LCC PS3616.E5555 B63 2018 (print)
    | DDC 813/.6—dc23
LC record available at https://lccn.loc.gov/2017060020

ISBN 978-1-5011-8904-3
ISBN 978-1-5011-8906-7 (ebook)

To

A-B-C

Anonymous, Boodi-nut, and Charlie Joe

Live it out like a god
Sure of immortal life, though you are in doubt . . .
If that doesn't make God proud of you,
Then God is nothing but gravitation,
Or sleep . . . the golden goal.

—Edgar Lee Masters, *Spoon River Anthology*

We walk in circles, so limited by our own anxieties
that we can no longer distinguish between true
and false, between the gangster's whim and the
purest ideal.

—Ingmar Bergman

CONTENTS

PART I

One day I will find the right words, and they will be simple.

—Jack Kerouac, *The Dharma Bums*

PRELUDE

TRANSCRIPT

SHERIFF'S BLOTTER – WOODVIEW COUNTY, CALIFORNIA
SEPTEMBER 15, 2001

"911 . . . What's your emergency?"

"Yes. My name is Helen Mayo. I live at 1531 Sweet Dog Lane. I don't know if I have an emergency, but I do have a new neighbor and I'm sorry if I just think he's [*loud dog barking renders caller unintelligible*]—Nicky, please!—I'm sorry that's just my little doggy—if I just think he's behaving strangely, and perhaps, the police would like to take a look, or maybe go and . . . you know, sniff it out. Sniff, chat, whatever it is that you do." [*more dog barking*]

"It's a little difficult to hear you, ma'am. Can you describe the strange behavior, please?"

"Well, it seems he's wrapping some kind of insulated wire around his house."

"Insulated wire, ma'am?"

"Yes, or maybe a clothesline. He's spooling it into his toolshed. I don't know his exact street number, but it's just two doors from me and across the street and I can see him from my kitchen window and, well . . . I don't know. I just think the police should be involved."

"Okay, ma'am. Thank you for your call. We'll go ahead and notify patrol."

"Thank you. Bye bye. [*renewed loud dog barking*] Who's a good boy-ee?"

....

SHERIFF'S BLOTTER – WOODVIEW COUNTY, CALIFORNIA
DECEMBER 7, 2003

Numerous residents of Upper Sweet Dog Lane reporting overgrowth of a neighbor's lawn. A 30-day notice has been posted.

....

SHERIFF'S BLOTTER – WOODVIEW COUNTY, CALIFORNIA
DECEMBER 23, 2003

Resident at 1528 Sweet Dog Lane was cited for illegal posting of placard admonishing, "International Airports Boast Morbid Mannequins at Duty Free."

At 2200 hrs., a patrol car, dispatched to the address, served the citation to the location. Resident was either not home or nonresponsive to officers. The citation was left at resident's door.

....

SHERIFF'S BLOTTER – WOODVIEW COUNTY, CALIFORNIA
DECEMBER 24, 2003

At 0634 hrs., Woodview County Sheriff's office was contacted by cited resident.

"Woodview Sheriff's Office."

"Yes, ma'am. I am resident 1528 Sweet Dog Lane and in receipt of a citation for illegal posting. To whom it may concern, it wasn't my sign."

(Without sufficient evidence to the contrary, citation was rescinded.)

SHERIFF'S BLOTTER – WOODVIEW COUNTY, CALIFORNIA
DECEMBER 29, 2003

Neighbors complain of excessive lawn mower noise—0300 hrs. When patrol arrived at scene, all was quiet. Scent of fresh cut grass permeating the air.

SHERIFF'S BLOTTER – WOODVIEW COUNTY, CALIFORNIA
DECEMBER 1, 2004

"911. What's your emergency?"

"Yes, this is Helen Mayo on Sweet Dog Lane."

"Yes, Ms. Mayo. What's your emergency?"

"Well, I just don't know. But that neighbor, I've called you about him before. He's cut his hair in a rather disturbing way."

"He's cut his hair, Ms. Mayo?"

"Yes, but I wouldn't bother you with a fashion, you know."

"No, I'm sure you wouldn't, ma'am. But you have to help me understand your concern."

"Well, this hairdo of his, it's something like a Nazi, or a woodshop teacher. And as you know, I'm not the only one on this street who has registered my concerns about this man. Despite numerous complaints or reports or what have you, I'm just baffled that you all have never actually engaged this gentleman. That you people haven't made any official law enforcement contacts. Forgive me if I . . . that with all his strange behavior and haircuts and all that . . . you know what I mean . . . I'm not saying he looks Arab, mind you. He's a white man. Anyone could see that, but I still think that the police should, well, you know . . . yes, sniff him out, just sniff that man out!"

....

STATION ONE

SEEKING HOMEOSTASIS IN
INHERENT HYPOCRISY

SUMMER 2016

Cactus Fields, a Low-Cost Home for Assisted Senior Living, looms like a large khaki-colored brick isolated against a backdrop of distant ambient light. Its draped windows and solitary silhouette sit in a seemingly endless desert tableau. Here it seems that the desert itself has been deserted.

And there they are, the brand-less beasts of yesteryear. Moist, sagging eyes, illuminated by the rarefied strobe of a passing car on the interstate. Behind the windows of the beige stucco building that sits behind a dilapidated, sporadically visited parking lot where brown weeds burst through fissures in the pavement, eight senior residents have been awakened by the power cut. They huddle side by side in plastic chairs. Portraiture of sagging faces falling in and out of indelicate light and shadow. Theirs, a blotchy batch of colorless dermal masks. That last life spark extracted from their oblivion, a reckoning of their uselessness in a world where branding is being. Bound by brutal boredom. Then . . .

mercy comes.

POP! POP! POP!

A chosen three down.

The elderly are being executed by a talented blunt force.

Gloved hands reconnect wires in a power box out back. Eight now reduced to five whose day will come. A dull white Pontiac ignites its engine, rolls over the fissures of weed onto the interstate and under its driver's breath, "It wasn't me."

STATION TWO

RECOLLECTIONS OF A TEENAGE CARNY

I t is the autumn of the age of reason.

Meet Bob Honey, resident of 1528 Sweet Dog Lane, a man who most often speaks of himself in the third person. A former fixed-wing shuttle operator, barge fireworks display purveyor, and one who made a killing in the septic tank–pumping industry by focusing on an exclusive clientele of Jehovah's Witnesses. After a brief monopoly on mail-order merkins and managerial stints at the Airborne Ordnance Maintenance Company and the Western Test Range, Bob regretted never attaining a real-estate license, and thereby never using his imagined tagline: "Buy a Honey of a property." He thought it might even make a good T-shirt slogan, dressed over his honey-bear heft, had his commitment to pocket protectors not overcomplicated the cut. Now, in his midfifties, Bob is a solitary man. If not a solid citizen, a stolid one.

Although he lives alone, it is Bob's perception that he wakes to his ex-wife, and to their speechless marriage each morning. Every night, he goes to bed alone quoting, "A-B-C / C-B-A . . . A-B-C / C-B-A . . ." The alphabet's first three, forward-back-repeat, in lieu of sheep. This is typically followed by a dreamless sleep. Come morning, as always, there she still seems to be. His silent ex-wife. Her chub and red hair. A small booger flopping, flittering, and fluttering like a carburetor valve backward and forward in her nostril with every breath in and out. A woman so cynical she doesn't understand the meaning of her favorite songs. One who concentered candy smells to her crevices in the self-objectification-seeking of every random man's desire. This pursuit outweighed even her own existence in any actual elation that life might otherwise offer. It is impossible for Bob, waking up all these mornings to her speechless misandry and fraudulently feminist superhero dreams. Impossible for him to not consider ligature strangulation. Droplets of gasoline ignited one by one, the stink of her burning flesh and affirmations of anguished screams. Ah, but when these considerations tickle the tumult of actionability, only then does he relinquish their delicious danger, and find himself buoyantly liberated to move away from the definitively empty bed.

Bob does know how to begin a day. One foot, then the other, into a pair of pants. A freshly laundered shirt. Open the gun safe in his garage, and transfer the wood-handled mallet of his prior evening's exercise from Clorox bucket to water-billeted brazier. Lock the safe, then whip up some fluffy eggs with cream. Cook 'em in the grease of crispy burning bacon, and get on with it. Yes, Bob is God's squared-away individual. He knows how to get up in the morning . . . and just do stuff.

The ex-wife his imagination re-committed to loathing each morning had actually left many years before, but she had never gone very far away. With money won in their divorce, she'd purchased an ice cream truck. The kind that cruises neighborhoods slowly, seeking out children with circus music broadcast through its PA system. That alternately haunting and annoying sound that conjures clowns, midgets, and stuffed animals. She'd taken up with another man, he the same euthanizer of compassion who'd represented her in court. Strangely, and to Bob's mind maliciously, they had bought into the high ground over Bob's adopted neighborhood, perched just a few short blocks away from Bob's post-divorce abode. Still, the upper end of Sweet Dog Lane she chooses *not* to cruise, in seeming avoidance of a direct encounter with Bob. After school in the winter and all day long in the summer would she peddle her frozen wares. The acoustics of Woodview are such that the distant circus music drifts torturously into Bob's ears for interminable hours. Hence, his life remains incessantly infused with her identity-infidelity, and her abhorrent ascensions to those constant salacious sessions of sexual solitaire she'd seen as self-regard. Ice cream trucks had become the bogeyman of his brain.

It hadn't always been that way.

A son of the San Joaquin Valley during the 1960s and early '70s, Bob rode a red Schwinn Stingray. Provided by the pale-blue-collar American neighborhood where Bob grew up was a window-shopper's gliding glance, while wheeling by the revealing open garages where muscle cars in multitudes marked time. Raised on blocks above oil pans, they were a sure indication of adolescents in Indochina. Riding past his heroes' homes, he often wondered if those recruited big brothers of his boyhood chums would live to claim their cars, or if they would return maimed, mindless, boxed, bannered, buried, or betrayed as the evening news portrayed. Bob's boyhood essence set him up for a separation from time, synergy, and social mores, leading him to acts of indelicacy, wounding words, and woeful whimsy that he himself would come to dread.

At its siren song, young Bob would sometimes cycle swiftly to chase down the ice cream truck (not unlike his ex-wife's), buy the Strawberry Shortcake Popsicle, then join the back of the pack of prepubescent punks, or more often ride alone through the neighborhood. Other times he'd go out to the river basin and throw homemade bombs off the Route 180 bridge. Molotov cocktails were preferable. Glass-bottled fuel, stuffed wick alight. Targeted, tossed, and arcing brightly. If you hit the paved riverbank close enough to the water's edge, the shattering bottle liberated a magnificent dispersal of high-octane accelerant upon the river's surface-drift. There and then, even little boys could create an impossible blaze, confound common sense, set a river alight, and amaze.

Out at the I-5 junction was an old mobile home park where Bobby-Eleven-Year-Old learned to smoke ovals on the porch of the tipsy trailer where the teenaged black chick lived with the Cowboy. Though small for his age, B-11 was thought a suburban danger-boy and had trouble making friends in his own age group. Cowboy was often an hour or more late leaving the trailer. He and his juvie Jemima had "realignin' to do to keep that damn trailer level on its gravel pad." As Cowboy'd finally appear, it was an appearance sweaty and ready to take the dutiful neighborhood boy on his septic tank–pumping runs. He'd teach "that little chump the tricks'a d'trade."

They'd saddle up in Cowboy's tank truck, ignition grinding into gear, as the black chick would emerge and stand wistfully at the screen door, her hair mussed and smile satisfied. Wearing only an oversized cowboy shirt, she'd warmly wave them off to work into the forearc.[1] Yep. Cowboy was one squared-away individual with his shit forever together . . .

Or so his young sidekick thought.

On a crisp and windy American morning in a 1960s November, the boy watched as a blue-suited tactical team took down his hero, grappling Cowboy to ground like a graven image. With Cowboy serving a state-imposed sentence for statutory stimulations and locked in stir, Bobby-Eleven-Year-Old turned his thoughts to her. That beautiful black girl, the one the neighbors had now branded a whore. He thought of her beauty and the lure of her shaved and shapely cinnamon sticks standing at the trailer's screen door. One way or another, he would fill ol' Cowboy's boots. But the booty of his desire had run from reputation, fleeing town, and fleeing with her, his *Summer of '42* dreams died like destiny's deadwood.

In that childhood, he revered *The Anarchist Cookbook*, a bible of bomb-making and mayhem for the misguided published in 1971. It misguided Bob to the heart of all good things. Potassium nitrate. What ranchers call saltpeter. They mix it into the salt lick of horses

---

1   The San Joaquin Valley sits between an oceanic trench and a volcanic arc, geologically determining that real estate a forearc.

when they don't want them to breed. Saltpeter is a proper devil. If you eat it, your wee wee won't work. But mix it up with a bit of sulfur and charcoal, or maybe a little sugar, and you have yourself the makings of a pretty pipe bomb. Magnesium ribbon, ignited by the flame tip of a Bunsen burner, illuminated brightly for a child's eyes. But more impressive was to cut a snip of it off, throw it in a test tube of hydrochloric acid, cover the mouth of the tube with a balloon, and watch it expand with pure hydrogen gas. Then tie the fucker off, get a long stick with a lit matchstick taped to the end of it, contact and ignite it into a fireball that harkens Hiroshima. With these tools (and a Christmas-gifted parabolic microphone), any hot-blooded young American could certainly save the world. Charlie Manson's world. The Vietcong's world. The Zodiac Killer's world. Bob's world.

To finance his fever for flame, Bob took employment as a kid-carny in local fairs and carnivals. It was in this occupation where he developed a flair for the mallet. Bob barked for the high striker, what is often called the "strong man's game." It consists of a heavy base and a long vertical tower. A groove runs along the tower's length. A puck sits at the tower's base beneath a lever, and at the top of the tower, a bell. If one strikes the lever with the mallet as-serting enough force, it will send the puck careening upward along the grooves to ring the bell. On Bob's, the tower ran the length of a fifteen-foot-high cut-out dragon, and the puck was heavy. Bob honed his own skills off-hours. While brute strength alone might'a been enough to ring the bell, it was really in finding the sweet spot of impact and torque of its swing where a mallet could be most malevolent. And the kid-carny barked:

"Be you knave or knight . . .

Come one! Come All!

COME-SLAY-THE DRAGON!!!"

Transitioning into adulthood, Bob, like any man, was introduced to evolving nemeses that began innocently enough with
an opposing neighborhood's militia of dirt-clod warriors, and
later graduated to the manipulations of mind mandated by a
green-grabbing media. It would be a challenge for Bob to enter
each new phase without noticing the pandering picnic of commercial waste offered in societal habituation. Bob knew the media
had limited success in telling the country *how* to think, but was
exemplary at telling it what to think *about*, to discuss, and to
value. If the hope of an individual seeking human connection is
to merge his or her mind's pursuit with the common interests of
society, they might soon find themselves shorn while crooning,
BAHHH-BAHHH-BILDERBERG.

Essentially a child bomber who'd dreamt of being a geolo-
gist, Bob had always found something just, righteous, or otherwise impulsively self-medicating to do, and he carried that habit
into his adult years. On geological terms, Bob initially concerned
himself only with the shine his lapidary equipment and tumbler
could bring to nearly any found stone. But upon some reflection,
it occurred to him that within the dust, bones, and petrification
of Paleocene sedimentary rock was held an egoless and truthful
history. Somewhere in the spaces of time, like the expanding and
contracting fissures in hardened earth sharply worn by millenni-
ums of moisture, it seemed mankind had traded truth for treachery,
both religious and commercial.

Branding is being! Branding is being! The algorithm of modern binary existentialism.

His childhood's fears of foreign wars and messianic maniacs, real and imagined, had developed into an ultra-violent skepticism toward the messaging and mediocrity of modern times. And, in opinions of morality, religion, politics, and science would he increasingly consider the possibility . . .

EVERYBODY

. . . ELSE

. . . IS

. . . WRONG.

By thirty, he'd gotten his grad degree. Physics, engineering, and a military CV. It was love that had gotten the better of Bob. Love of women. Love of innocence. And lust for his own maddening mind's doubt.

He'd spent such a significant several years in the septic specialization industry, one so full of pathogens, worms, and protozoa that if left untreated would come to represent a present public health crisis. Like love or innocence, it's not a business so easy in which to get one's footing. The very soil upon which one stands contains forty million bacterial cells per single gram of soil. It is jam-packed with microbes that if used properly will break down the pathogens. Now, while sanitarians decide design, Bob found his forte in pumping and baffle replacements. Despite a deep understanding of depth soil's vertical separation to the bottom of the drain field, then to the top of the ground water's restrictive layer, and also a relatively acute sense of sludge layers leading to scum layers, to the effluents leaked to leech fields, there was one sentence from a Sunday sermon that had stuck out to Bob from the basic precepts of Jehovah's Witnesses, who had built their "system of belief and practice from the raw material."

That phrase had summoned in him the singular entrepreneurial interest in isolating those churchers' investment in his septic services as a pumper. This had kept him far from the branding crowd and the technological advances of social indulgence so circuitously enslaving those more supple of skin. Bob kept his skin supple on the work site with latex gloves.

Paired with an extraordinary auditory augmentation efficiency that came to Bob in equal parts handy and haunting (more on that anon), his engineering acumen was unparalleled. His knowledge and experience, secured through a surgical sensibility toward his vocation, complemented Bob's skill set–specific capacity for reverse engineering. Almost without effort could Bob synthesize civilian architecture. By identifying where urine and feces fell, and its storage system's size, design, and placement (especially where gravity systems are employed), he could mentally x-ray the interior of a building simply by observing its exterior. This, he thought, had application in human systems analysis as well. Such thinking could render a man's spirit and personality severe. His ability wasn't brandable, but it was Bob. Bob Honey. A man with a Middle Eastern mission in mind.

STATION THREE

EPHEMERALLY DISARMED

Bob traveled to Baghdad during the holiday season of 2003 to explore opportunities in the waste management sector. If he could get an exclusive with the new Shia-backed power base, he might package a turnkey operation from septic tank installation to pumping and disposal. This had projections far exceeding the earnings from his monopoly on Jehovah's Witnesses in the eighties.

After a surface-to-air missile had clipped the left wingtip of a DHL Express plane shortly after takeoff from Baghdad on a November afternoon, all commercial flights into or out of the city had been suspended. Bob worked his way onto a flight operated by Air Serv International, its seats exclusively at the service of NGOs and other humanitarians of note. The *Afrikani* pilot had been trained by a former employee of Bob's own (now defunct) fixed-wing shuttle business. He did Bob a solid for seven hundred in cash,

securing him a seat out of Amman. Bob and six certified humanitarians went wheels up at 0400. He leaned his forehead against his
seat's portside window, gazing into the night as they streaked the
ninety minutes of flight. He caught himself humming the chorus
of OutKast's "Bombs Over Baghdad." His limited awareness of
popular music was such that all hip-hop and rap sounding songs
were to his knowledge from a black band called Two-Pack.

In a distant desert darkness, towers descend into black.
Vapors of Iraqi oil burn like floating fires
atop of their black night blended stacks.
As carbon dioxide poisoning purities escalate war,
chemically charged coloring surrealizes sunsets galore.

It was into such a sunset that the plane approached Saddam International Airport.[2] All passengers on the eight-seat aircraft were
instructed to strap in tight and expect a g-force sensation caused
by the corkscrew landing necessary to confuse and evade any
heat-seeking surface-to-air missiles fired by insurgents. The pilot
employed the hard-banking spiral landing technique. Bob knew
that corkscrews often take their toll on more touristic tummies.
Halfway through the corkscrew, two of the terrified aid-workers
aboard succumbed to its strain and torque, spontaneously regur-
gitating in barf that boomeranged back into their own faces. Bob
sighed as the suffocating stench consumed the cabin. His olfactory
system offended, he held his breath for five complete minutes until

---

2   now Baghdad International Airport

the plane, as if riding the rifling of barrel spirals, pitched level and landed, taxied, then opened its door. Bob hastily exited and breathed the new morning's Muslim air.

He'd checked in to the Rose Petal Hotel, outside the Green Zone and behind its own ineffectual barricades, blast walls, and barbed wire. He was to meet with ministers and blackmarketeers serving under the auspices of Ahmed Chalabi, El Jefe of the Iraqi National Congress. Chalabi, a US seducer, pawn, and all-around purveyor of bad science. Chalabi, a fugitive from Jordan who'd fled a case of fraud, hiding in the trunk of a car and stealing his way to Baghdad.

In black linen suit, businessman shoes, and a pressed white shirt, Bob dressed and exited the Rose Petal Hotel on the night of the arranged meeting. He hot-wired a sitting taxi, but ran out of gas on his way to the INC compound in the Mansour district. He began to walk along Haifa Street, where he stumbled upon a sidewalk sandbagged gun emplacement, and simultaneously sized up the sixty-cal barrel protruding from its position. Without warning, Bob found himself molested by a team of rogue indig military contractors wielding Kalashnikovs and well-traveled Khyber Pass Copies.[3] "Moonlighting Kurds," he thought them. After they'd gone through his pockets and waistband, they caught a wood-handled and leather-wrapped mallet he'd concealed in a shoulder holster. When they attempted to seize it, he steadfastly and physically refused. Avoiding an escalation of scuffle, the Arabic

---

3   black-market bootleg M4-series rifles built by gunsmiths in the semiautonomous tribal region between Afghanistan and Pakistan

mono-linguists radioed their dutiful dragoman. That's when the New Guineans arrived and took jurisdictional control.

There can be no wiggle room on the facts.

FACT: Grass-skirted Guineans patrolled and protected corporate sites on the streets of Baghdad following the Shock and Awe[4] campaign of March 2003. And, what better mechanism of terror than to embed grass-skirted cadres of cannibals within these ghostly ghettos of the Arabian night? Right?

Gold, copper, oil, natural gas . . . Mining interests and exploratory missions of bullish buccaneers in New Guinea brought an appetite to build paramilitary and security capacity on that Oceanian island. The indigenous model was spearheaded by a head-shrinking entrepreneurial tribesman named Loodstar (himself, a turncoat to Indonesian oppression). Loodstar established the Papua Academy of Urban and Guerrilla Warfare in the early '90s and, after the October 2000 attack on a US warship in a Yemeni harbor, he had the forethought to supplement tactical war-fighting and security strategies with Arabic and English language syllabuses.

Splitting their days between Academy training, subsistence farming, and archaic rituals, the Guineans became a force to be reckoned with. Corporations that sought to protect their inter-

---

4   "Shock and Awe" is a term commonly remembered as a moniker meant
to bolster the visceral muscularity and charismatic propagation of a violent
campaign in order to titillate for the TV turnouts back home. As a matter of
diligent fact, "Shock and Awe" is not a media-baiting term or a term invented
by the media for the purpose of baiting their viewers. It's a military term for
actions of rapid dominance. A term for an action meant to introduce such
apocalyptic terror in its first strike as to bring its enemy into rapid psychological collapse, inducing surrender.

ests in the Levant at discount rates skipped over Blackwater and DynCorp and went straight to these snake and bird tribesmen. In the early 2000s, the five-sided puzzle palace[5] had an autonomous private contracting budget[6] of $20 million a year. Dollars dispersed with impunity to contracting companies operating without elected oversight. Their employees, often good eggs doing the dangerous and difficult work, and, just as often, assholes in need of attitude adjustments. A grab bag of seasoned former soldiers, security specialists, and small-town truck drivers toiling for tax-free tender,[7] with government gifting grandly to these corporate gunslingers, be they of guts or greed. Loodstar fit both bills and sealed a couple of contracts quickly. And so began the peregrination of tribal ops to contract in Iraq with *spear-ian* flare, grass skirts, and bare feet.

With that Baghdad evening's chorus of *crackity-crack* percussion from long-barrel volleys exchanged in purlieu, the rhythm of multiple mosques' Calls to Prayer, and the occasional ominous off-stage *okónkolo* of ill-tempered ordnance, Bob sat soothingly sung to with his newfound brothers-in-arms; the tribesmen and he in a blast-blackened office space, its roof reduced to rubble by a car bomb the night prior, leaving the stars and the Iraqi moon to illuminate their Turkish tea, freshly slaughtered chicken, and Tawi, a red fruit indigenous to New Guinea.

---

5   the Pentagon
6   This was separate and apart from the no-bid outsourcing contracts that tallied
     bills in the billions. Halliburton's KBR, etc.
7   While US soldiers were paid downward of $60,000 annually and taxed on
     their gross income, their private counterparts were paid by their same puzzle
     palace $100,000 tax-free.

Bob's relationship with people, much like his relationship to food, had become largely independent of that which might pleasure his palate. He'd long since lost touch with a diversified appetite for either. But there was something in a people like these Guineans. They, whose first contact with the modern world and its corruptions had only been a short half century earlier when missionaries became more culturally constructive communicators with cannibals. In them, Bob found a subsistence-based serenity and grace of purpose. It did occur to him (as a private joke with himself) that were the chickens they chewed not in such high supply, he might have found himself on the menu. By the time the hookah was fired up to be shared, his newfound sense of belonging left him socially, if ephemerally, disarmed. As such, he began to share tales of his failed relationships with redheads, cowboys, neighbors, and needs.

Though he'd come to Baghdad with sewers and septic tanks on his mind, Bob would leave emboldened, not as an entrepreneur, but as a fresh recruit to a program sublimely suited to society's solitary men. That chance meeting with the tribesman on Haifa Street in 2003 had, in its discovery of kindred spiritude, graduated our traveler from his personal practice of practical patriotic vigilante-ism to a sanctioned occupational status. A brand-new job for Bob!

When he woke on that stone floor of the bombed-out Baghdad office space as morning came, Bob found himself chimney-sweep filthy and abandoned by Guinean brethren to their predawn re-deployment. Inside his passport, he found they'd left behind mission codes for him. These were the digits he would henceforth

press into a burner phone whenever he sought a contract. He also found all that was left in his ankle-sock hideaway: a grand total of ten US dollars. Now he would have to make his way to Jordan by road: a fourteen-hour, $400 cab trip. Despite having been intermittently successful in rather diverse businesses, his minimal money-management skills had always restricted him to cash-only transactions. He neither invested nor took lines of credit. As a traveler, he would often find that he was prone to under-budgeting his various escapades and found himself scrambling to access a bank. Filthied but un-frazzled, he road-marched to Saddam City,[8] where he was able to find a cell phone vendor from whom he could purchase ten tele-minutes with his remaining ten dollars. He called the Arab-accented POC[9] he'd intended to meet with the night before.

With every bank on the Baathist boulevard bombed, he was ultimately able to get a $400 marker from the man at the Chalabi compound. He took it and hired a taxi to Jordan. Fuel shortages in the oil-rich country led cabdrivers to spend entire days in pump station lines. But not Wader, the abaya-bearing cabbie he encountered. For one thing, Wader's fuel gauge was on the blink, so, assessing its levels and range was for Wader a constant and challenging guessing game he engaged with glee. Rather than linger in lengthy lines, Wader would make the long trek through the Anbar Province, buying one precarious liter at a time along the way from the black-market boys of Fallujah and Ramadi. Wader's

---

8   later renamed Sadr City
9   Point of Contact

whimsy for wheeling Wahhabist roadways was unsettling to his white war-zone passenger. But, to his credit, Wader had a way with fuel-wagers. Gauge on the blink though it was, he deposited this California commuter with punctuality for his flight out of Amman.

Back stateside, among Bob's neighbors was the bouffant boasting, burdensome Helen Mayo. During his often and extended absences from Woodview during the years following 2003, she'd satisfied the ire of her snoopy suspicions by making a point of walking her Chihuahua, Nicky, by his house, eagerly encouraging Nicky to do his business there on his lawn. There is a karma in this world. It can't always be understood, but in 2016 it would put on quite a show.

STATION FOUR

THE SCOTTSDALE PROGRAM

In the American state of Arizona, Scottsdale Senior Services offers a wide range of fitness, recreation, and leisure opportunities.
This and its dry air make Scottsdale one of the preeminent retirement communities in America.

There is little but coincidence to connect Scottsdale, Arizona, to
Papua New Guinea; Scottsdale's dry climate contradicts the clammy
calescent of New Guinean condensation. It had nonetheless come to
the attention of the New Guinean intelligence apparatus, Loodstar
in particular, that a covert contract of international implementation
was in the offing. It was called the Scottsdale Program, named with
nods to both the city of Scottsdale itself and to the Phoenix Program of the early 1970s, with which the CIA sought to devastate the
military infrastructure of the Vietcong in South Vietnam through a
series of targeted assassinations on its military commanders.

The Scottsdale Project's origin at the Heritage Foundation was sold on the back of separate studies from Rand Corp and McKinsey and Company at the behest of the Rendon Group public relations firm. The project was adopted by NSA, who believed that in an era of globalization, an internationally unbranded generation of seniors threatened to bleed human progress and market development dry. Neutralizing pushback against the program from the pharmaceutical lobby were those in the EPA's covert section, whose data concluded that the extermination of high-flatulence populations[10] would lower levels of ozone-depleting methane. This would be a boon to industry! On an atmospheric real-estate basis, it would allow industrialists to freely occupy the terminated tenant's toxic-absorption zone. In simple language, an air-grab wherein air-polluting companies could expand production with a zero-sum exacerbation of environmental impact. A sort-of sewer swap offered for the emission of one in the expulsion of the other. No harm. No foul. No fogies. FANTASTIC!

An interesting note on this: Studies show that kangaroos expel no methane while providing lean and tasty meat. And as a result, in the prevailing portfolio of per capita killing, the flatulent and significantly unbranded elderly under the Scottsdale Program were second only to sweet meat kangaroo among biped land mammals being culled.

Our mallet-wielding American male has never, despite some deliberate delving, satisfactorily distinguished between Scottsdale's direct government implementation status and that of a shadow

---

10   old people

enterprise. It is not clear to him whether the White House is, or is not, in the sodality of Scottsdale's reporting chain. His only substantive certainty is that practical patriotic tasks of triage are everyone's responsibility, and that American taxpayer money is paid to career operatives in stacks of small denominations. Bimonthly, a Janet-Jet[11] (white plane, red stringer, no tail number) drops in on random remote runways of red states where Scottsdale's clandestine operatives, each wearing an identity-shielding gorilla mask, have been called to greet it. As the air stairs meet the apes, a fetching functionary of the confederacy descends, handing each a stack of singles, congenerous to mail calls in conflict zones.

Where others might dream activities such as Bob's, in Bob's living of them, he finds himself dreamless in sleep. It isn't such a different experience, he thinks, than what the hordes who so alienate him encounter themselves in their daylight's consciousness. In his mission-gap moments he studies the skin of his arms. "Is that me I see? Whose arms are thee?" In these moments of physical self-study, Bob feels foreign, separate from his own body. The brown-black hair upon his outer forearm. The smooth-skin hairlessness of his inner, where whenever a stray might sprout, he'd bite it out.

Bob rarely receives callers, though once in a very long while might someone invade Bob's solitude. Typically, these instances are self-regulated to afternoons in sunny weather. Perhaps Bob's house, despite its common, single-leveled smallness, presents itself

11   Janet is a de facto name for a small fleet of government aircraft. Janet is said to be an acronym for Just Another Non-Existent Terminal.

as an oddity or as in some way a fright to anyone who is not diligently disposed to a sunny state of mind. When a knock comes at
the door, it almost always comes timidly.

It is late afternoon on just such a day, following just such a
knock, when Bob first opens the door to the gruesome burger-
meat grind of a face so ravaged by its history of adolescent acne that
its pits and protrusions catch sharp shadows where horizontal light
sneaks below his hat's brim. The man appears roughly Bob's age, if
not a few years his senior. The two of them share blank stares for
several seconds of silence. Strangers on pause, yet as if awaiting the
tines, tuning forks, and violet rays of Tesla's coil. Might this, their
meeting on this day, be that resonant transformer?![12] Then, "Allow
me to introduce myself. Spurley Cultier. You're Bob Honey?"

Bob nods.

"I knew by your address," Spurley says.

Bob nods again.

"May I come in?" asks Spurley.

Bob nods a third time. Then, in an impulse most alien to his
personal history, he allows the portly stranger into his home, shyly
gesturing him toward the small living room. Cultier takes up the
table-end chair and Bob sits centered on the couch.

"French?" Bob asks.

"American," says Cultier. "What do you do, Bob?"

Bob ponders, puzzled. Then, "Just . . . stuff. What do you do,
Mr. Cult-E-A?"

---

12   Inductor of coupling or magnetic phase synchronous coupling. The most basic
     resonant inductive coupling consists of one drive coil on the primary side and
     one resonant circuit on the secondary side (parallel resonant frequency).

"I'm an investigative journalist, Bob."

When Bob chuckles, it is a muted, guttural guffaw. Audible, though never intended so.

Spurley asks, "Do you think that's funny?"

Bob shakes his head, then, "So, you ask people questions?"

"Yes, Bob."

"And they give you answers?"

"Sometimes they do, Bob."

"Do you believe their answers?"

"Sometimes I do, Bob."

"Not me," Bob says. "I don't believe anybody's answers."

"Can I believe yours, Bob?"

"No, sir. I don't know if I ever really tell the truth, much. I wonder sometimes if truth might be more habit than virtue."

"Yes," says Spurley. "The practice of honesty has a gray hue."

"So why do you ask questions, Mr. Cultier?"

"Good question, Bob. It's a heck of a good question, indeed. I'm glad you asked me that question. I'm gonna go ahead and try to answer it, Bob. Your neighbors, I noticed on the sheriff's blotter, have made several, how can I say, interesting observations and inquiries of you to the local sheriff's office over these many years."

Bob nods almost imperceptibly.

"Are you aware of that?" asks Spurley.

Bob's toolbox never included feigned puzzlement.

"The optics are suspicious?" he offers. "Hmm, yes. I have noticed department patrols slowing as they pass my home."

"You got it, Bob!" says Spurley. "That's what it is. Your word, *optics*."

"Mr. Cultier, why do you pronounce your name Cult-E-A if you're American?"

"How would you have me pronounce it, Bob?"

Blushing, Bob says, "It's none of my business, sir."

"Let me ask you, Bob, would you be amenable to my visiting again—and please call me Spurley."

Bob thinks long and hard. Something seemingly ancient and primal inside him is peeking out and may testify to a turning point in his socially exiled existence. In systems theory, one small thing leads to another. The water, the plants, the photosynthesis, and the eventuality of bloom. In punctuated equilibrium,[13] it is like an earthquake, and suddenly everything changes. If one is not adaptable, catastrophic systems failure will occur. Bob begins to recognize the punctuated equilibrium being visited upon him, and will not allow a catastrophic systems failure. Spurley, it seems, might be the right vessel, at the right time, akin to the geological philosophy that one's search for ores and fuels serves as a means to a practical end. Spurley Cultier may have materialized as a facilitator to Bob's rebirth of being. Voluntary value-added to algorithms of the new norm. Bob will initially seek to adapt.

"Perhaps we could meet out," suggests Spurley, "McDonald's might be a good location, on Hedgepoint Road?"

No arches for Bob. "I'd prefer my home . . . Spurley."

"Fair enough," says Spurley, rising from his chair. "Shall we say Wednesday, four p.m.?"

---

13   biological theory proposing that once species appear in fossil record they will become stable with little evolutionary change; stasis

"I'm sometimes not here," Bob says, in an effort at fair warning.

"Yes, well, we'll talk about that," Spurley replies as he moves to the door. "I'll be by Wednesday at four, and if you're here, we can talk a bit more."

Bob nods but never rises from the couch. Spurley lets himself out and Bob watches through the picture window as Spurley takes note of the Pontiac in the driveway, then drives away in a Prius. The silent type. For the next several hours, Bob will not move a muscle. But he can feel an unusual pounding in his heart, and a slight shortening of his breath.

It is on that couch where Bob feels safest, almost embraced. And in his stillness, there, on that day and into the evening, return his visions of Annie. Ah that girl. That shining young face. Bob has always experienced life as an aspiration to dullness with dignity, absent as much deceit as possible. He has no tolerance for advertising. Annie had been that one brief break in the weather where his dullness dazzled a dame. If Annie advertises, Bob thinks, it is without falseness. Or, at least less falseness than others. And after all, Bob is not prone to question himself in that single matter of the heart that Annie reflected, the waking rarity that Annie had become to him.

They'd met on a park bench one day during Bob's surveillance of elderly lawn bowlers. " 'Ello," offered a velvet voice. One look at her standing above him in that park and Bob felt a relaxing of his joints. She may have been young. She may have even been *too young*. But Bob never bothered himself with those distinctions. Annie had alopecia and wore an astonishing wig. Bob could barely feel it false with his hands and wouldn't worry it if he could. Simply the fact that her baldness was covered in blonde and not red made him love her head. Effervescence lived in her every cellular expression, and she had spizzerinctum to spare. They sat and talked, or rather, she did. They had a brief love affair, or rather he did. What a magical vagina, Bob thought, after exploring it for hours. Hairless, but magical. Bob had never considered himself an aesthete, but he did look long and hard for things that might disturb him. Though Annie was by any man's measure an exquisite aquiline Sheila, it was in the absence of disturbance that beauty was defined for Bob. It had begun that very day, after strolling to his house from the park. They sat silently on his comfort couch. A look between them.

Off came the clothing and on came their effortless ease of communication where vagaries landed literally, and silences as voluminous volumes. Never one for psychosexual infantilism or pedophilic fantasy, after their sex he said, "Good vagina. Maybe more Vietnam." "More Vietnam?" she asked. "Is it a bit urban, *sugar*? You're looking for some jungle?" Bob nodded. "Okay," she said, "I'll put on my little merkin piece next time."

"Okay," said Bob. "As you were.[14] Thank you. Thank you very much."

"Are you into tantric sex, Bob Honey?"

"Too much reading," said the so slotted *sugar*.

"Agreed," Annie said. And so went their discussion and his continued examination of her body. And so went on and off the

---

14   standard military command literally meaning, "return to your previous posture"

romance for a brief few months. Until inevitably off she went, and forever away, but not without the occasional text message from her travels, or perhaps one image from a select telephonic photo diary. Fifteen pictures to date. The most recent, an unvarnished snap of a twelve-inch and girthy black dildo, which appeared to have been discarded on a city sidewalk beside a casino poker chip and some publicly planted greenery. It came with a simple note, "Greetings from Las Vegas! I'm with the girls!"

Bob had found fundamentally foreknowledged form in the way Annie giggled at his apparent brooding and solitude. In her generation's world, Adderall and advertisers' chickens had come home to roost. Bob felt from feline millennials the transmissions of Instagrams blitzingly blazing from all directions. The sensation of Roman arrows careening chaotically within his skull. The tracer round ammunition of human selves anonymously exposed. No one spoke to anyone, and when they did, it was more about those anthropomorphic arrows than it was the natural air of organically human traverse. That air, that life, again, so unceremoniously sidelined by a generation bent to uninvent the wheel of love, and so willfully inattentive to control computations or surveillance. An age group so lost to letters and steeped in transactional sex, it seemed of them that they distinguished little between an active orgasm and an acted one. So quickly might Annie cum that he'd try thinking of chocolate bananas, cotton candy, and chugging trains to ward off consciousness of her detachment and perhaps to delay his own ejaculation in hopes of making hers definitively real and defiantly human. Yet, to no avail.

Whenever he felt these collisions of incubus and succubus, he punched his way out of the proletariat with the purposeful inputting of covert codes, thereby drawing distraction through Scottsdale deployments, dodging the ambush of innocents astray, evading the viscount vogue of Viagratic assaults on virtual vaginas, or worse, falling passively into prosaic pastimes. Instead, he would quake the elderly in all corners. POP goes the weasel! Bob's mallet would speak. He knew his destiny's turn.

She had taught him well with her smile, cerulean eyes, and the little thoughts she thought of him, when she thought them. Ahh, that girl and the glistening between her legs . . . Schooling him in the forward movement of herself and her contemporaries. A cultural momentum undeniable as gravity. As irrefutable as the generational inversion of human expertise she so embodied. In Bob's defiance, he had found himself, against advisement, awaiting things that had already passed, leaving him to face that harshest prospect of all: that he must give up on the only thing he really wanted. He'd hungered to tell her all his secrets, but became one of them instead.

He knew a likely pipe-dream better than most; she had never led him on, and sure enough, his maturity of tellurian years alone had given him a huge head-start in his feelings for her, and he never expected her to catch up on her own. With any encouragement, he'd've backtracked till he had her hand in his. Had a present hand in his past. He imagined that often, being encouraged, her hand in his . . . as the ever-present image of her knowing deep blues beckoning softly before him.

He had dropped her at departures that last time. Then the aircraft engines revved, wheels left ground, and his world's atmosphere became host to a new variant of air, absent the sweetness of her breath. Yet mercifully, also absent those arrows of post-adolescents careening through lower altitudes. He takes comfort that her smile, like heaven's shield, will keep her safe, warm . . . and wild.

STATION FIVE

BIG COCK

Several days have passed since Spurley Cultier's visit. Bob catches himself standing by his posted kitchen calendar, staring at the days with distraction. He sees that this is Tuesday. Sixteen hundred hours. On the following day, Spurley Cultier intended a second visit at about this time. Bob had noted it on the calendar. He steps up to the refrigerator, opens it, pulls out a fresh packet of hot dogs, exits the house, gets into his Pontiac, rocks the mirror dice, and hits the road. This will be a mission of the medicinal sort. One man's act of absurdity may be another's substitute for solace. Bob is indeed a man of moral purpose; yet, this does not prevent him from worshiping at the altar of Emerson's espousal, "foolish consistency is the hobgoblin of little minds." So aggressively arrogant, Bob thinks, is the man or woman who lacks the will to adjust or compromise in the service of a greater good. He thinks of things political. Their lefts, rights, and mutual wrongs. The cynical lack of substance to their reciprocal unequivocals. For Bob, one plus one still equals two.

Thems the facts as he feels them.

The leftists, he thinks, see themselves as idealists and intellectuals. Hence they forsake inclusion of a *right*, be it in gaming, greed, or pragmatism. This forsaking by either side contributes nothing to a result, real or ideal.

"What works" (be that question or solution) is the be-all/end-all for Bob. Tonight, it is Bob's turn to practice his conscience's preaching and find a place of value for the contrived sexual objects played with by a party not his own. He will create a ritual around them. Dancing away demons in the defiance of their danger.

Results, Bob thinks, are the religion of an active mind. Like Tesla standing between his coils, he will be a bridge of universal energy. "Moral sh'moral, you kill coral!" he comments to critics unseen. Concern over carbon emissions has played a role in leading Bob to stray from the magnificence of fire to the malevolence of the mallet. Increasingly mindful of his carbon footprint, he has started calculating the g/km[15] of his burnings and blowings-up of old persons and other things, putting himself on a socially responsible quota of containment.

With Annie's photographic chronicle of Vegas parading in his mind, Bob drives across the Mojave in search of any and all inti-

---

15   g/km: grams per kilometer

macies of inanimacies. From the fifteen stations of love, he'll start with that large black dildo ditched street-side those many months earlier. Once the information is captured, Bob's internal after-action brief prompts his provision of personal protocols and the rules of engagement moving forward. He had long doubled as his own compliance officer. Armed with Oscar Mayer wieners, white birthday candles, and an X-Acto knife, he is only three hours on the hunt in Vegas when he sniffs it out from under a hedge, using Annie's sidewalk photo for reference. He removes one of his socks, uses it as a glove, and picks up the big black unit. He then drives forty klicks into the Moapa Indian Reservation to memorialize his find in ceremony.

At midnight on the reservation, Bob is assaulted by animism in the swirling surround of desert and stars. He claws out a hole in the ground, and sticks the dildo's base into it. With the X-Acto knife, he slices a small sliver peehole into its tippy top, then inserts the bottom of a white birthday candle into the peehole, lights it, and slightly adjusts its direction toward the North Star. A flash ignition of fumes due to the degradation of the silicone bursts from the dildo's undershaft, creating hands of flame that seemingly reach to cup Bob's face and pull him in. The schlong burns fast and hot as he listens for echoes of Emerson granting ozone amnesty. He hasn't even gotten the first hot dog out of the package, much less cooked it, before the whole cock melts with the wanton "Why me?" of the Wicked Witch, from prick to puddle. New protocols were called for. Defeated, Bob looks toward space, and begins to sing, "*Oh, I wish I were an Oscar Mayer wiener, that is what I'd truly like to be . . . cause if I were an Oscar Mayer wiener, everyone would be in love with me . . .*"

BRANDING IS BEING!

With desert duty done, a return to house, home, and freshly cut green grass. Bob's overseas endeavors generally allowed his Woodview lawn the overgrowth of non-volitional neglect. He remembered an incident back in December of 2003, when arriving home around midnight from a trip overseas to a notice from the county clerk threatening penalties. After picking up the poo left by you know who, he'd gone straight to his toolshed and pulled out his 1966 Briggs and Stratton winder-start mower. He flipped the winding hinge and entertained its rotational clicks as he spun it. Then hitting the electric starter, it burped and sputtered into action.

The younger Bob had treasured his chores and none more than the mechanized mission provided by the mower. He was always meticulous to the wheel line. No better groundskeeper anywhere in the San Joaquin Valley. With mowing, Bob could be king of his own domain, and no domain ever had such a fine moment as that when the fragrance of fresh cut grass filled its air. On these occasions, he enjoyed the splendor of its focus facilitated by following the streetlight-shadowed edges as they caught lines luminescencing levels between what he'd mowed and would mow. Later, with the machine back safely in the shed, Bob showered and put himself to bed. He clicked on the TV and watched a whirl of news: American media coverage on the Middle East.

In the battle within Bob's brain, media sources created a chaos of overload. A marketed, manipulated assault on retention. History books did the same. All heirs to Herodotus.[16] The Western

---

16   father of Greek historians nicknamed the Father of Lies

developed world, considered so rich in pride and possibility, more often than not kills beautiful things in the human heart. Pride, he believed a pleasure better suited to Orientals and peasants than to those of the West, who'd come to so commonly detach love from infinity, while ubiquitously clinging with cowardice to the fearful fabricated prides and prejudices of yesteryear. How is it possible for a white American to calculate positive or negative impacts on Middle Eastern matters? One could either passively advocate medievalism and intellectual poverty or at best bow to moderate governments that tolerate a measure of both. The only remaining option: intervention. There didn't seem much room to maneuver in the cradle of civilization, and our senses now so systematically suppose savagery. Hence, Orientalism[17] is most probably a topic best observed by Orientals.

In these instances, Bob would make himself switch off the television and close his eyes. Insomnia would generally get the better of him. He should never ever compromise a Zen cultivated by lawn mowing. He should never ever again let his brain be flagellated by trifling with the tube. But he'd done it and his powerful peace was gone. Evaporated. To reconcile this, he'd try considering his affliction of sleeplessness as one closer to a familiar fold: daytime made a practical demand upon most working people. But it was de facto in the night's contentment of consensus isolation where Bob felt most a part of the bigger world's boastful best. In those wee hours wide awake, a reprieve. He wouldn't need worry

---

17   Orientalism is the belittling way in which the West considers Easterners, those peoples of Asia, North Africa, and the Middle East.

the incoming tremors transmitted by his ex-wife's ice cream truck and its tedious trickling of cold cunt soup. His mind could clear all angst and echo of emotion and lend itself to conjure a glorious girl. This, even before the onset of an actual Annie in his orbit . . .

This glorious girl would sit before him naked in a chair. She didn't pose her breasts. It seemed she didn't pose anything. Her beauty was independent of her lovely face and body, and neither in need of vanity to boost or question its shine. It swam out from her eyes in wonder, whimsy, and depth of quotient jest. Her skepticism of moral convention mightily complex.

On the night in memory, that of late-night lawn-leveling, just as he felt he might drift, he heard the approach of a vehicle outside his bedroom window at 0320 hrs., followed by the reflections of red and blue lights strobing through his blinds. He listened, heard the muted squawk of a police radio. Its pause, its "all quiet," and its pull-away. Finally, its seceded sounds' surrender to his beautifully cut lawn's lingering symphony of silence.

That had not been a night for sleeping, much like this night's nocturnal navigation from a burning big cock in the desert, in clothes stinking from silicon soot. By dawn, he's made it home. Wired in Woodview, one last chore to wind down.

After parking the Pontiac and closing the garage door behind him, he moves to the gun safe. Opens it and counts out a thousand one-dollar bills from a pile stacked high inside. He re-secures the safe and goes back to his bedroom, where amongst the clutter of his bedside drawer, he finds a blank envelope. Wearing latex gloves, he inserts the thousand dollars into the envelope, then moves to the kitchen, where he wipes its glue strip wet with a damp sponge beside his kitchen sink, seals it, stamps it similarly, and addresses it to the Woodview chapter of the ASPCA. He puts his feet into his Wallabees, walks out to his mailbox, puts the post inside, and raises the metal flag for pickup. The sun rises on a new day. Back inside the house, he puts on a CD and collapses into bed. Phil Ochs sings,

I cried when they shot Medgar Evers
Tears ran down my spine
I cried when they shot Mr. Kennedy
as though I'd lost a father of mine
But Malcolm X got what was coming
He got what he asked for this time
So love me, love me, love me, I'm a liberal

STATION SIX

A PORTRAIT OF ENTROPY

"I see you're unshaven, Bob. You look a little tired. A bit black-circled. May I ask what you've been doing with yourself?"

Spurley Cultier sits once again in Bob's living room at the table end chair, with Bob center couch. Bob is becoming dubious of Cultier. Perhaps ol' Spurley is a spy. Bob often thought how consistently the intelligence community lacked intelligence. They spell "data" with an eight and call it code. It occurs to him that there is nothing covert about a man with a knife collection (they all seem to have exotic knife collections).

Bob inquires, "Knives?"

"Knives??" asks Spurley.

"A knife collection. Do you have one?"

Spurley's smile goes squirrelly.

"I'm an investigative journalist, Bob."

"That's right," Bob says, "you ask questions. I think if questions are asked of politicians, they should be regarding any acts of cruelty upon animals in their youth. The problem is—"

"They would lie?" Spurley interjects.

"This seems to me the problem," says Bob as he excuses himself to the kitchen, pours himself a glass of water, and adds a maraschino cherry. From where he stands, he can see that Spurley has put on a pair of cheaters and is scribbling several notes on a pad with a number-two pencil. Bob considers eyeglasses a terrific invention. It's a wonder one can wear something on one's face with such negligible discomfort or distraction. Bob takes a brief detour inside his own brain, then calls to Spurley, "Water and a maraschino cherry?" Without turning his head, Spurley nods affirmatively. Bob pours him a glass, popping a cherry into it.

"If it's all right with you, Bob," Spurley says, "let's discuss a few knowns. You know, known knowns. I have been taking a great interest in you of late."

Bob nods.

"Looks like you spent some time in the Middle East. What was it? A few short weeks before they grabbed Saddam? Helluva time to travel Iraq, Bob."

"The trip related to septic tanks," Bob says. "Honey, Inc."

"Honey, Inc.?" asks Spurley.

"Yes," says Bob. "With a 'C.' Inc.—Incorporated."

Spurley scribbles a note. "I feel like we're getting to the meat and potatoes here, Bob."

"You're hungry?" asks Bob.

"The meat and potatoes. The meat and potatoes. You're talking to me about your business."

"It's my business."

"I understand you feel that way, Bob. But with this many complaints . . . do you know Helen Mayo—neighbor of yours?"

"I know the floor plan of her house, and that her fear of USOs[18] had her flee a beach community in the sixties."

"The floor plan of her house?"

"Yes. I take walks and have a talented ear."

"Do you, Bob? A talented ear, huh?"

"Yes, I think so. I take walks, and on my walks I often pass her home. She has a yapping dog, you know. A Chihuahua. Over the years, I've been able to surmise a sense of stairwell connections to corridors connecting rooms front and others back. The measurements of floors to ceiling. The echoes of Chihuahua yaps bouncing off bathroom porcelain. All of these collected echo-placements and levels of sound draw pictures in my head."

"Fascinating, Bob," says Spurley.

"It's just something I find I'm able to do."

"That's quite a gift, Bob."

"Mmm," mutters Bob.

"Mmm hmm," mutters Spurley. "And what do you do with those images made from sound?"

"Just stuff I guess. It's something I could do since I was a boy."

"Ahh."

Bob nods and gazes off as Spurley pauses unsurreptitiously

---

18 Unidentified Submerged Objects

scribbling a series of notes. In Bob, the lead on paper of Spurley's pencil's scratch stimulates extrastriate sub-cortex synergies in
his mammalian brain. His auditory augmentation of reality systems renders words in the rear of his retina with visual vibrations.
Scratch by scratch, letter by letter, word by word did Bob's internal
cinema display Spurley's glib taunts of font:

C-l-a-i-m-s . . . o-t-h-e-r-w-o-r-l-d-l-y n-a-r-c-i-s-s-i-s-t-i-c s-k-i-l-l

s-e-t-s. D-o-e-s t-h-i-s f-o-o-l r-e-a-l-l-y b-e-l-i-e-v-e C-h-i-h-u-a-

h-u-a-s c-a-n b-a-r-k o-u-t t-h-e f-l-o-o-r p-l-a-n-s o-f

h-o-u-s-e-s? D-o-e-s h-e r-e-a-l-l-y t-h-i-n-k h-e-'s f-o-o-l-i-n-g

o-l' S-p-u-r-l? I-S H-E T-R-Y-I-N-G T-O S-E-L-L M-E H-E-'S O-N

T-H-E S-P-E-C-T-R-U-M?

Then Spurley speaks. "You know she watches your place quite
a bit. She's got you leaving at all kinds of funny hours and often
for long periods of time."

As lights rise and exit doors open, Bob's cerebrum sacks its
cinema and steps back into the world. "Did you say something?"
he asks.

"I was asking about Helen Mayo's observation that you're
often away from home for long periods of time."

"Hmmm. Mayo . . . Spurley, my house needs airing out.
Sometimes a place can get stale harboring the body of a man."

"The body of a man, Bob? The body of a man? Now we're
cookin'."

Spurley waits for Bob to break.

But Bob says calmly, "Yes, Spurley. The body of a man. Mine.

Sometimes the house wants its space." Spurley's disappointment is evident.

After a deep breath he continues his questioning, "Maybe you keep a diary, Bob?"

Bob shakes his head.

"Maybe you keep one somewhere, huh, Bob?"

"Do you write nice things about people, Spurley? Or mean things?"

Spurley seems caught off guard by this question. As he appears to search for a sensible response, Bob interrupts his silence.

"I'm not having fun, Spurley. The house and I need a little space."

Reluctantly, Spurley recognizes that he has pushed hard enough for one day.

"Understood, Bob. A man should never overstay his welcome."

"Thank you, Spurley," Bob says.

"You're welcome, Bob. I'll be checking back in with you."

Spurley chugs his glass of water, leaving the cherry at the bottom.

"I'm gonna leave you the cherry, Bob. You might need it."

Bob nods. Spurley goes out the door, peruses the Pontiac, and proceeds silently away in his Prius.

Bob's cell phone suddenly sings out its ringtone.

Raindrops are falling on my head
And just like the guy whose feet are too big for his bed
Nothing seems to fit . . .

He pulls the phone from his back pocket and accepts the call. Three beeps from the other end. Bob responds, entering a three-digit code. Two beeps, followed by a secondary four-digit code. Onto his display: "Thousand Oaks Elderly Care Park, 205 Gallavant Road, Thousand Oaks 96789."

Bob enters his garage, double-locks its doors from the inside, opens his safe, and removes the mallet from the water can, heavy with moisture. He towel-dries it, holsters it, closes the safe, and re-enters the house. He shits, showers, and shaves, puts on some khaki pants, a laundered shirt, and an old pair of Wallabees. When the Wallabee hits the Pontiac's accelerator, the Pontiac set its course for the outer reach of Woodview's extended megalopolis, Thousand Oaks.

In the common room of the Thousand Oaks Elderly Care Park, the Wonderful Wednesday Aerobics Club is being led by a five-foot-four, seventy-eight-year-old woman in a pink ballet tutu, dark green stockings, and runners. Bob has a clear bead on them from his shaded position under an oak parked between the golf course and the croquet lawn. It is common for Bob during the observation phase to muse on the company's selection process. In this case, certainly aerobics may itself be a brand, and the tutu individualism of its *instructor* might as well associate her with said brand. But Bob has spent enough time, in fact, thousands of hours, studying animations of double-rod pendulums,[19] and knows that

---

19   a physical system exhibiting rich dynamic behavior and strong insensitivity to initial conditions

in their aspiration to claim aerobic exercise, they are only clutter-
ing the world further, with chaos physics.

This is the thing about brands and beauty. They cannot be
randomly claimed. They demand continuous polish and they rest
on a greedy system of valuation that provides those who pursue
them a fraudulent sense of comfort. Out there in Thousand Oaks,
if there was any pattern to the shared psychology of its residents, it
was a random one, waged by an encouragement of their decrepit
circulatory systems in an effort to prolong their own useless lives
and comforts. Pathetic, Bob thinks. Holdouts to hedonistic pro-
crastination. Awkward and inconvenient.

Red lipstick has no place in exercise. And two full feet above
the waistline of the tutu, her crinkled lipsticked lips, her sun-
spotted face, her over-joyously little twinkling eyes. He knows how
she saw herself. A Pop Granny, he thinks. Have I got a pop for her.

When class breaks, Bob wheels the Pontiac away and finds a
local market, where the purveyor makes sandwiches from day-old
bread. He asks the bread be toasted, the bacon and lettuce both
crisp, one slice of tomato, and plenty of mayo to nullify the tomato's acidic effect.

Outside the market, Bob sits in a filtered luminescence reflected by the day-end's fuchsian light as he watches the bloodred
sunset from within the capsule of his Pontiac. He hoists himself
into the back seat, then slivers into janitor's overalls, the mallet
holstered inside, beneath his armpit. When night falls, the Pontiac's back door creaks open. Step-by-step he walks the quarter
mile back to the elderly home. Along the way, he absentmindedly
picks up discarded bottle caps, rolling them like raconteurs, figure

flipping them through his fingers before sending them soaring with the nimble snap of his thumb. There are cigarette butts and burned-out blunts. The smoggy smell in the night air's humidity. It brings him back to those trailer park days of Cowboy and Jemima, and the rollicking reminiscences of riding his red Schwinn after bombing the river. It is a happy feeling—nostalgic.

With the tutu on her nightstand, the aerobics instructor glosses her washed face with Nivea cream. Her failing eyes, unable to note the puddles of that white cream unabsorbed that remains hiding in the troughs and crinkles of sun- and age-ravaged skin. God's portrait of entropy. She puts on her nightwear, gets into her little childlike bed, and sets off to sleep with dreams of Cuban bar boys.

The janitor pays a visit. POP! goes the weasel.

Returning to the Pontiac, Bob slides in a CD, and the mirror dice return wobbling toward Woodview, Phil Ochs's voice sings,

"I am the masculine American man. I kill therefore I am."

STATION SEVEN

SEXUAL DUNGEONS

"**B**lunt Force Trauma" headlines the newspaper as it slaps the stoop of Bob's door in the morning. Bob wakes to the sound of its delivery's clap, and before him, a booger flake flutters in *her* nostril like a hummingbird's wing. The stink of *her* morning breath far too human, flawed, and plaque-ish. In the canine world, only small dogs can mimic such a monster. Small dogs, indeed, are capable of fishy breath. Not so, big dogs, who at their worst may expirate the yeasty odor of stale bread. They are predictable in that way. There is no tragic chaos to them. Bob is particularly moved by, and admiring of, wolves for their gait and monogamy. In his heart, he knows himself to be a hybrid. Not a "dawg," but, yes a dog. A house pet with wolf blood. It takes a special bitch to elicit his commitment. He'd found and delivered his best to a few, most often to women of chub and red hair. He's been bitten in the throat each time nonetheless and considers the word "bitch" too flattering for anything without canine creds. These he considers only as ugly, ungenerous souls.[20] Women who operated in direct impingement,[21] blasting out one's best bullets, and expelling their casings to the curb. Powder-burned, hollowed, and primer struck. Provisions should be material. I am neither provision nor material, Bob thinks, and thinks back to the chubby fuckin' redhead whose ghost still whorishly haunts his bed.

The booger continues its hummingbird-wing thing till Bob is nearly nauseated. Though he dreams assassination upon phrases like "me time" and "my truth," Bob certainly feels no obligation to defile himself in conversation, or indulge continued study of a face only beautiful by the standard of mathematical symmetry. He silently extracts himself from the emotional isothermality of his bed and plods naked to the bathroom. There, sitting on the standard toilet, he lets his imagination drift in its discovery of ancient faces within the patterns of the marble wall. On any given day, perhaps based on the firing of synapses, or the level of reflected light, one could find an infinite materialization of faces in marble. Haunted faces, gargoyles, the wise and the soulful. Marble, like sedimentary rock, holds greater truths than any man. And man, does Bob know it.

Before taking a morning walk, he makes a brief detour into his garage, where he recalibrates the Pontiac's odometer less the mileage accumulated to/from Thousand Oaks, round-trip. Com-

---

20 cunts
21 a type of gas operation for a firearm that directs gas from a fired cartridge directly into the bolt carrier or slide assembly to cycle the action and expel the casing

pleting this task, he steps over the morning paper to take his daily constitutional. As his Wallabees meet the tarmac of Sweet Dog Lane, Bob's sixth sense for amateur urban hides[22] and the distinct bark of a Chihuahua draw his attention to the upstairs window of a neighbor's home. There he detects Helen Mayo observing him from behind a blind in an upstairs window. He stops in his tracks and stares at the blind for one . . . then two . . . then three full minutes. Eventually the blind is pushed aside. Helen Mayo chooses to skirmish Bob in a stare-down. They glare at one another. He, because the sun bounce is glary. She, with suspicion and bitterness. Both of them oblivious to the sound of a helicopter falling in emergency reverse autorotation. Suddenly, the helicopter falls full force from the sky, crashing through Helen's roof, obliterating Helen, and bursting into a frightful fireball. Her now-flaming Chihuahua named Nicky runs from the wreckage blind, ablaze, and barking throughout his meteoric dash across the street before crashing headfirst into the curb, where his incineration croaks, crisps, and collapses him curbside with the immediacy of a grand piano's lid prop's pull. No more barking. Bob considers his options. A futile rescue effort from a house fire fully involved? Or GET OFF THE X?[23]

When the fire department arrives, Bob watches from his stoop as aviation investigators tape off the scene around Helen's house. Local police and media arrive. Even PETA volunteers show to collect the compact canine's cadaver. Power hoses turn black smoke

---

22 camouflaged sniper position for urban settings
23 moving off the line of force, or away from crosshairs

into white. And Spurley's little Prius pulls up before Bob's house. Spurley parks and approaches Bob.

"Hi, Bob," Spurley says.

"Spurley," says Bob.

The local TV station and its overly tanned and toothy male reporter have set a camera and tripod in the center of Sweet Dog Lane, panning the crime scene to land on the toothy-tan one, whose backdrop is the wreckage of Helen Mayo's smoldering house. The reporter's pulpy piercing voice clearly audible on the porch where Bob and Spurley stand: "Officials are not prepared with a determination that this has been an act of terrorism. The deceased pilot is burned beyond recognition— Sorry, folks! This is graphic stuff . . . kids go find your mommies. What authorities *have* verified is that the pilot's remains were found with a charred turban on its head. As for Helen Mayo, they did Sikh and find remains. Get it? Sikh! Get it?? No? That's all. On a beautiful Sunni day, did I say *Sunni*? I meant sunny. In either case, Shia beauty! Your man in the field, Cheeky Chuck."

"Quite a little drama," says Spurley with an expression bordering on ironic scorn.

"Bad optics?" asks Bob.

"Seems to be a lot of that in your orbit these days," Spurley responds.

"Orbit, hmmm," mumbles Bob.

Back in Bob's living room, the two men return to their established positions. Spurley launches in.

"Here's the thing, Bob. The folks I work for had asked me to pick a random male living in my own community for a feature focusing on an American man unknown to his own neighborhood—yes, I've gone door-to-door here on Sweet Dog and not'a'one knows ya. This may sound a bit esoteric, but stay with me on it. You know the sort. The individualist. The archetype. Mailer's White Negro. That fella on the block, nobody knows him. He's a loner. Antisocial. Maybe he has a dark secret? You know what I mean? Something seemingly sinister. A scheme. A schedule. A sexual dungeon. That kinda thing."

Bob takes exceptional offense. "I don't have a sexual dungeon, Spurley!"

"No, no. I wasn't insinuating that, Bob."

"I'm not a Negro either, or sinister, or whatever you said."

"Relax, Bob. I know that. Of course. All I'm saying is, I went ahead and asked a few questions in the neighborhood and of the local police, and there seemed to be only one fella continually drawing my attention. And that fella is the same fella whose timing, be it inconvenient or coincidental, had him taking his morning walk at just the right moment to observe the very neighbor who had most often filed complaints with the police about him, being obliterated by a rapidly descended helicopter . . . Like you said . . . optics. Together, we can alter perception."

Bob nods.

"You spend a lot of time on your own, don't you, Bob? You got a gal?"

Bob nods. From the distance, he begins to hear the circus music of his ex-wife's ice cream truck.

"Where is she, Bob? Where's your gal?"

"I don't know, Spurley. I haven't seen her in a long time. I get messages from her sometimes, er, pictures, you know? Will you excuse me, Spurley? I've got some things I gotta do."

"Like what, Bob?"

"Just . . . stuff."

As he walks Spurley out, the music of the ice cream truck attenuates in amplitude. Bob moves back into his house, leaving Spurley on the stoop, listening through the door as Spurley goes on his way. In his bedroom, Bob sits on the edge of his bed and opens the drawer of the bedside table. In the clutter of the drawer, he finds a picture. It is of him and Annie. The only time the two of them had ever traveled together was when Bob had been hired by a Bolivarian state to orchestrate a Cinco de Julio pyrotechnic display from a barge off the Venezuelan island of Isla de Margarita. The picture is, along with Bob's passport and California driver's license, one of only three photographs he knows to exist of himself. It is of the two of them, him and Annie, the ocean, the palms, and the hammock they shared on a Wednesday afternoon. Annie, a vision. Eyebrow bare and beauty so fair. But Bob? His best face of good fortune feels forced as a festive felony mug shot, yet mercifully sympathized by the drooled bit of banana that rested obliviously beneath his lower lip.

He carefully replaces the photo at the bottom of the drawer in one corner, sliding camouflaging clutter over the top of it. From there, he moves back to the closed toilet seat, sits on it, and lets his eyes wander the marble, like a map of human history. A metaphoric rock of re-crystalized carbonate minerals, the calcite or dolomite. He pulls the cell phone from his pocket and googles

"Gabriel's Oboe."[24] As it comes up, he presses play and lets the
music make the marble and its faces of time dance before him. The
oboe and strings develop the faces of primitive man. In the pre-
lude to the climb rises a deformed face of Christ, bleeding into the
Crusades. Gargoyles gasp and birth monkeys creep into lava-lamp
articulation. A piccolo flute's solo calms Cretans and lepers arriving three at a time. The French horns, like conquered Nazis,
in any color of marble do their eyes reflect blue, while Plutarch's
men of *Parallel Lives* barter bluster. Then caught by the image of a
smoking boy with blue eyes wide, flash-framed through a fissure,
asking, "What's up, Mr. America?" And in the requiem . . . Bob is
born, grieving in granular detail. Cued are the choral cascades and
faces of fallen friends when, in its conclusion, would Bob weep.

And so he does, as the marble of mankind dances before him,
from the beginning of humankind to the creation of Annie's face.
Hers, like KEPA,[25] ballistically blasting away the battle scars of Bob's
heart. The blubber tears burst from his eyes and snivel from his nose
into the magic whisper of Morricone's flute, until the entire form of
Annie molds itself outward from the marble in dance. As her appa-
rition releases her falling hair, the clip she'd removed falls into Bob's
agile hand. He closes his fingers and grips it. Bob utters to her dancing form, "I want to be drowned a little bit by the baby soft hair at
the nape of your neck. The lenience of your lips in the sun. There's
just too much oxygen here. I need to know more about peeling bananas from the bottom, but I also want to do that in tropical places.

---

24   Ennio Morricone's orchestral masterpiece
25   Kinetic Energy Penetrating Ammunition

There are these extraordinary feelings I get, Annie, after vacuuming my house, but, even they don't compare to you. You're too banging beautiful for words, and are far too precious to ever see hurt. In any way you will ever allow me to love you, I will. I'll be vacuuming till the next time I see you." Bob wipes his tears as the form of Annie is reabsorbed by the wall. Still, the hair clip remains cupped and real as royalty in his unfurling hand.

Where has life gone? Where is its data on previous engagements?[26] Bob is fifty-six and numbness dominates his day. As a creature adept at selective memory, he'll sometimes fill gaps by speaking aloud to himself. "Woodview, California, has trees and birds. Woodview, California, has *treason* birds. I am Bob Honey, surrounded by trees and birds." Surrounded by treason. Treason to love, to creation, to art and authenticity. He stands, returns to the bedroom, flips on his television. A former professional athlete is modeling underwear. A famous movie star is driving a marquee sedan above cliffs and sea. A game show host selling cell phones, and all so proud in their specimen standing and justification for the self-charity cha-ching and bling. Branding is being born, as the elderly drive us down. Bob stands between the ages. Torn, broken, co-opted, a mercenary for marketing in treason to thy self.

He tries to medicate against the slow-coming dark and devastating dawn of depression. He begins with a child's word trick. "Whatever." Then moves on. "It doesn't matter." "Have a sense of humor for God's sake. It doesn't matter! It doesn't matter!"

---

26   aka DOPE. A process used by precision rifle shooters to log, track, and access information specific to his or her weapon's behavioral history and unique machining.

The splitter. The splatter.

The 'I love you's' without any truths . . . or does it matter?

When everything is replaceable,

all of us traceable, and memories erasable.

Nothing matters in vodka or tonic,

in the absence of ironic, in exhibitionism so chronic.

Nothing matters if we let it be so.

If no isn't no.

And yes, is just something we say until we go.

Nothing, that is,

but blood flow.

And maybe a little while later

nuclear glow.

STATION EIGHT

INSECT HOMICIDE 2016

Sometimes Bob would hear Annie's voice in a whispered tone, even long before he'd met her.

"I love the way you love me, my Bob-beam. You know it. And I know it. The music of an ice cream truck sells sweetness, but its wares are cold and fattening . . ."

She'd hit the nail on the head. FLASH: Four-year-old Bob with a bowl-and-bangs haircut crawls under his young mother's hospital bed. Her head is shaven and marked, mapped for imminently invasive incision. His mother calls out with weakened words, "Bobby . . . my little Bobby, let me see you. What are you doing, darling, under my bed?" He claims he's hiding from the sun. That the glare through the open vertical blinds of the hospital room window had hit him at her door. Says his eyes are watering, not tearing. The TV is selling erotic perfume while the blood of an aneurism is exploding inside his mother's brain. His father holds his mother's hand. Asks his wife if she might like to try the perfume . . .

Advertising. Bob's albatross. His burden least benign. Its way of sanctioning ego and deceit. The transparent greed of it. Its saturation of popular imagery. His sense of a malignant mass amnesia that has been welcomed by the worms among us into social acceptance like a creeper in the night. A country so marketed into madness. Manipulated and aghast. Now comes into craze this ubiquitous *shock and dismay* while witnessing fellow citizens fall witlessly to fascist forays.

Though dumbification clearly plays a leading role in herd immunity to wisdom, Bob, a man so significantly self-educated, attributes this populist lapse more to a forfeiture of the electorate's youth's truths. A lapse in recognizing the basic complexity of each human's history of shame and isolation. Humanity's unending game of hide-and-seek with its own soul, reconditioned to downtick its hiders' heart rates and seek safe passage in the comforts and valuations of common celebrityism. This, the new American dream, where arrogance is charisma, character is complaint, and gray, a color of tolerance no longer tolerated.

Bob's ex-wife's ice cream vending business has become a sensation. She's done interviews and has her picture in the local paper, bought herself and her lover a big fancy house on the upscale side of town. Expanded her fleet and therefore expanded the territory of sound that Bob cannot escape.

In his nightmare, he is married to her still. Stemming from the previous day's circus music–infused air, and his drive home from

the market, when several insects had exploded on his windscreen,
the nightmare begins with memories sweet as nicotine.

She tastes so good, you roll her in your mouth.
Then it kills with cancer, and life goes south.
Through insect homicide, all these towns,
all seen before.
The interstate abandon
while she neglects a fragile core.
Cacophonous castration is such a fuckless bore.
Insect homicide. I'm here not sure for what.
For insect homicide.
Then the ceiling is large and ornate.
Doors creek over posh Austrian slate.
She lies sleeping in the big plush bed.
Last night's champagne eyes are this morning's red.
Life, full of strangers.
Words like interviews *and* phoners.
Life, where what is sacred is only for the crowd.
Life, lived in circus music played aloud.
Nothing is private nor special in the notoriety of frozen sweets.
Decay is all around.
Men are monsters, we all know that.
So, Bob sits still and listens
for the sound of her vengeful bat.
And the religions of success that succeed only
In the hatred of god.

"Oh, my Bob-beam, drifting in such a terrible dream. It's you and not the ice cream vendor who need clarity and cream."

Bob jolts awake.

It hadn't been a pleasant dream but that he'd dreamt at all leads Bob to recommit to the seeking of social connectivity. He's been hoping to have that impulse plussed. He's seen it in others but it has always been elusive to him. A purpose-driven soul, the soul of his purpose had remained elusive too. He'd been close once, to a fulfillment. Its formula perishing in a mathematical mind-fuck, whilst endeavoring to make faces from fractals, effigies by equation in evidence of great spirits. And by these means, he'd come so close to rendering the visual equation manifesting the face of God. He lamentably lost a thread of his thoughts and cursed his human bandwidth deficiencies in numerical retention, those that had left portions of his prognosis to simply perish from consciousness like dreams *had*, or jokes *heard*. So, as one does, he picked anew from what drew him at any given time. Bob's life, almost less human than dog, is a life lived as his own pet. He takes himself for walks, roams into adventure, and protects his master. One could always count on a dog to follow his nose. After some fluffy eggs and bacon, Bob takes his morning constitutional.

Out on Sweet Dog Lane, he takes to the street. The trees of treason and the worker bee ice cream trucks look down, superintending the landscape of Woodview, viewing Bob's walk and broadcasting John Lennon (as sometimes trees do) in the unrevealed post-apocalyptic neighborhoods of the dwindling middle classes.

Mommy-daddy
Yo-Yo
yummies
Little Bobby's
broken toy—
Nineteen sixty's
promise broken
Battered brilliance of an
unspoken boy—
Patriots poundcakes
drowned the dreams of coital
comfort joys—
Where did all the great loves go?
Lasting life's . . .
less than lasting toys.

As soon as you're born they make you feel small,

Bob stepped with his right, and then his left.

By giving you no time instead of it all,

He pulls his watch from his wrist and drops it to the street. A neighbor boy rides up on a red Schwinn and lifts it.

Till the pain is so big you feel nothing at all,

Blooming with berries, birds besiege Mountain Ash as Bob bounds forward, chin up.

A working-class hero is something to be,
They hurt you at home and they hit you at school,
They hate you if you're clever and they despise a fool,

His lace comes undone and nearly trips him.

Till you're so fucking crazy you can't follow their rules,
A working-class hero is something to be,
When they've tortured and scared you for twenty-odd years,
Then they expect you to pick a career

As he turns down a perpendicular street, he locks eyes with his ex-wife cruising the next block in her ice cream truck, thawing liquids leaking languidly from her cargo-cabin. She pauses at the intersection, glaring at Bob. Hers, a face that creates and collects ignorance, arrogantly assimilating it as common knowledge. Her expression on this day is fraught with the same disgust she showed whenever Bob chewed the ice of his cocktails on their evenings out. In her sophomore sensibility, it had never occurred to her that his liquor intake solely served as a delivery system to his interest in ingesting ice. Now, she sells ice cream for money.

Funny.

As she turns back to the wheel, she reveals her body's silhouette. A physique surgically enhanced since last seen by Bob. Had she traded the mythology of her modesty for cosmetic self-awareness?

Getting older in America is tough on a woman; seeing what she'll do to avoid it is tough on a man. While there can be nothing better than doing business with an *established firm*, Bob often thought, the maintenance of femininity cannot be measured by masquerade, masculinization, or marvels man-made. To Bob, his ex seems all. The lovechild of unobtainium and transparent aluminum, she has more baggage than inventory in her physical excesses and ice cream trucks. As she accelerates away, Bob feels incommodiously un-inebriated.

When you can't really function you're so full of fear,
A working-class hero is something to be,
Keep you doped with religion and sex and TV,
And you think you're so clever and classless and free,

Behind decorative gabion walls, an elderly neighbor sits centurion on his porch watching Bob with surreptitious soupçon. Bob sees this. Feels fucked by his own face.

But you're still fucking peasants as far as I can see,
A working-class hero is something to be,

Now, over the topography of Woodview he sees his ex-wife's continuing navigation toward higher elevations of town.

There's room at the top they are telling you still,
But first you must learn how to smile as you kill,
If you want to be like the folks on the hill,
A working-class hero is something to be,

A kind-eyed danger-dog appears before Bob. Its eyes lock with his. But for only a moment as if to say, "I've been waiting for you." The dog cuts into an alley and Bob feels pulled toward it as if by a huge Neodymium magnet.

If you want to be a hero, well just follow me

A break in flux density[27] and the dog skitters away. A spontaneous breeze picks up a page of morning news flying into Bob's face, wrapping it into momentary blindness. Bob takes a last few futilely following steps and is reminded of the last friend he'd ever made. That man in the middle of the sea.

---

27   the magnitude of a magnetic, electric, or other flux passing through a unit area

STATION NINE

RELIGIOUS TOURISM 2015

The shimmers, booms, sparkles, and arcing sprays of color, the virtual sky dance that had been Bob's pyrotechnic display at Isla de Margarita, Venezuela, had been a sensation and gained the attention of progressive governments throughout the region. They clamored for his services. The winning bidder, Bolivia, was land-locked since it lost its coast to Chile during the War of the Pacific. But its determined Indian president had designated Lake Titicaca as a showplace for environmental studies during the weeklong National Quinoa Festival. Bob would airfreight his pyrotechnic barge and land fourteen thousand feet above sea level in La Paz, chew a little coca leaf to thin the blood, then truck his wares to the lake and the fireworks christening of the president's showplace. En route, his eyes followed "Wanted" posters that pictured a Hasidic Jew from Brooklyn who had been imprisoned on a bogus money-laundering charge. It was strange to see a man with a yarmulke and sidelocks on a South American wanted poster. Even stranger posted roadside on the trees of a Bolivian jungle. Evidently, the fellow had escaped his prison and was now a wandering . . . fugitive.

After Bob once again impressed a presiding figure with fireworks, he opted to make his way to the port town of Arica in northern Chile to raise a sail on the barge, and take it north by sea back to California. With a Peruvian trucking company and portolan in pocket, he traversed the disputed territory[28] to the sea. Armed with a tent, scuba dive kit, plenty of fuel, and an outboard, Bob would brave the swells and perhaps get in some choice diving. Only two miles off the Chilean shore, a maritime map identified a tasty deep-water canyon. Bob anchored the barge to the canyon's shallow edge some seventy-five feet below surface, geared up, then plunged into the crevasse.

Bob found peace in the darkest depths, and swam beneath bioluminescent fish. In the company of clusterwink snails, *Abraliopsis* squid, and the symbiotic bacteria of anglerfish, the ocean, it could be said, was Bob's only friend. In this place, where Bob offered the water no disturbance, more floating with the current than swimming. And where it took no disturbance to initiate luminescence, unlike at the surface where all luminescence disturbed him, and seemed itself born of disturbance. The only expectation of a man at that depth was to see, breathe, and monitor his own heart rate. There were no billboards, no televisions, no Instagram messages,

---

28   The Attacama border dispute between Chile and Bolivia currently leaves Bolivia landlocked.

no Annie, no ex-wife. Not even the echoes of mayhem from a mallet muted. No, the sea was Neptune's land, and Bob its most serene servant. With his hypoxic nitrous mix dwindling, it was time to make the slow ascent to the surface. As the chasm's diminishing darkness led to refracted shafts of rainbow sunlight, he rose, then broke the surface and took a big gasp of fresh air. Spent, he pulled his butt up onto the edge of the barge, facing out and flippers in the water, pulled off his mask and the top of his atmospheric dive suit, shut off his regulator, and released the clasps of his tanks. The weight off his back, Bob stared into the sun until a voice startled him. He turned to see a frantic, water-drenched Jew pointing Bob's own spear gun directly at Bob.

"Who dju?!"[29] demanded the man. "You're vid Bolivian intelligence?! Dju vid cartel?! Judiciary?! Tell me now, who dju?!"

"I'm Bob. Bob Honey."

"Dju American?!" barked the man.

Bob nodded.

"Vat ver you doing down d'ere?"[30]

"Fish. Looking at fish. Floating around."

The man asked, "Shvimming?"

"Well, yes, I guess so. I was swimming. Diving."

"I need to get out of here!" said the man.

"Where did you come from?"

"I tunneled outta da prizon. Ran inta'da jungle. Ran tru da trees to da road, den caught a bus'h to da border. Den da beach.

---

29   Jew-speak for "Who are you?"
30   Jew-speak for "What were you doing down there?"

I never loiyned how to shvim, but I made it, dju SHONS-OF-BITCHES!! I dog-paddled, LIKE A DOG!"

Bob's thought process inadvertently led to a private notion being shared aloud.

"I feel like a dog sometimes," he said.

These words seemed to calm the man, and Bob may have met his amphibological match!

"Vere are you goink, Bob?"

Bob told him he'd be attempting to sail the barge all the way to California, stopping intermittently at tasty scuba diving locations. The man lowered the spear gun with apologies and introduced himself.

"I'm Fischel, Bob. Take me vid you."

In the days navigating north through international waters, Fischel and Bob found a simpatico camaraderie. Fischel whined on about the wife that had left him during his long Bolivian imprisonment. While often taxed by the diatribes, Bob's brain read between the lines and found solidarity in Fischel's anguish. But more than that, Fischel was a creature stripped of all conditioning, religious and civil, suffering the inherent indignity of years as the lone American in Bolivia's worst prison, and doing so on the trumped-up charges made by corrupt officials had left him animalistic, almost primitive—qualities that fed into Bob's briefly burgeoning emotional wheelhouse. Perhaps too, timing had played its role in Bob's recognition of friendly feelings. After all, Fischel was his first creature contact since the bioluminescents from below. Though a non-swimmer, this dog-paddling Jew offered courage to the sea, and Bob and he were able to switch shifts sailing northward. This allowed each some tent-time, their typically restless sleeps immunized by the lulling sea.

A week into their journey, and well into the international waters off Cabo San Lucas, Fischel napped away his Shabbat for Moses as Bob, in his scuba gear, explored the ocean's depths and listened to his heart's proof of life. When he ascended, he felt a slight disturbance in the water. Looking up, he first thought he was discovering the underbelly of a humpback whale, but in fact, after a bit more ascent, it became clear the barge was being approached by the hull of a large vessel.

Bob worried for Fischel, that it might be pursuers, bounty hunters, Mexican mercenaries. As he surfaced, he encountered a strange phenomenon. The architecture of sound defining this place, which, at the time of his submergence, had been a diligence of seagull songs and wind-lapped water, had changed. Now upon his ascent, its audio architecture had been superseded by reverberative subwoofers and an up-tempo Mexican disco tune. And in this otherworldly wall of mercurial sound did Bob find Fischel, dirty dancing atop the barge with a gyrating and bikini-clad curiosity of cryptozoology. The music came blasting from the yacht that had twinned with the barge. Fischel's chimera-esque dance partner, red lipstick smeared on her teeth, held a shot of tequila high above her head. Seeing Bob swim toward the barge, her smile widened, the streak of lipstick on her teeth, magnified. Her face vaguely familiar to Bob from channel surfing stables of semi-famous Televisa tarts. This goat-backed lioness began to hoot like a bruxism bedeviled banshee. She stalked toward Bob offering one hand to boost him up onto the barge while exclaiming, "If

you don't drink our TEQUILA, we'll throw you under the barge!"
She laughed with vagarious vulgarity. Thinking herself funny, she
flung a shot of tequila into Bob's facemask. Its drippings streamed
glass to mouth. He licked its cheap perfumes with salty lips and
grimaced. Though feeling conspicuously out of place, he took the
shifty chimera's hand and boarded the barge, where he dropped his
gear. Fischel said to him, "Bobby BOIIIII-EEEEE! Glab yourshelf
a shenyorvita. It's FIESTA time!" So much for Shabbat.

Standing at the yacht hull above the christened inscription,
Plata o Plomo, was a man of diminutive stature and imposing pres-
ence. "Amigo!" he called out to Bob below. Bob smelled the waft
of seasoned food. The man on the hull took note, pointing at the
ladder where the bikini-clad chimera's cellulite sloveled its way up.
"Come on board, amigos! We'll eat!"

In a palatial maritime dining cabin, Bob and Fischel found
themselves enjoying a bounty of marvelous Mexican cuisine. There
were pretty girls dancing, servants serving, and machine gun–
toting bodyguards scanning the skies and chumming the friendly
sea to frenzy sharks for fun and folly. Bob and Fischel sat with
their host of diminutive stature. They drank from a bottle of tequila boasting the image of a winged woman resembling Fischel's
dancing partner and branded with the name Tequila-Mockingbird.
Common interests shared at the table included tunnel technology.
Bob had often thought to dig tunnels under his home. Escapeways
for the endlessly imaginable scenarios of need, and as a boy, had
delighted in his own hand and shovel excavations of underground
forts. He'd take days or weeks to dig 8 x 8 x 8 foot holes in a square.
Worm-slicing, rock-cutting, water-revealing holes. He had found

an affinity with the underground. And on this basis alone, the yacht fiesta was for him, a bountiful if bewildering occasion.

CRACKITY-CRACKITY-CRACK!   Sudden   automatic gunfire interrupted the easy feeling of the fête. One of the boatman's bodyguards had sighted a hovering drone and shot it out of the sky. It was time for the yacht's host to be on his way. His crew hustled him into a DeepWorker[31] and he parted from Bob and Fischel politely, "Adios, amigos!" As the hatch of the miniature sub was sealed over him, he was craned and splash-dropped overboard. As the submerging DeepWorker disappeared the diminutive drug dealer into the depths, the tequila-wielding chimera howled desperately after it, "*Mi amor! Mi amor! Llévame contigo!*"

With that, the bottle of Tequila-Mockingbird was blasted from her hand by the gunfire of fast-approaching vessels, its bitter brew splashing in broken glass at her feet. As the captain of the cumbersome yacht geared up engines in a futile effort to flee, Bob and Fischel bounded onto Bob's barge. With a hurried pull of the outboard cord, they plotted their way away from *Plata o Plomo*, staying hidden within the convenient cover of a blue-black smoke cloud the bigger boat had dispersed when her captain hit its multistroke's choke. The crew of that cocaine-cruiser was left behind to combat with Mexican marines. And the awful chimera? She sharted agave shimmering spirits and shifted shit-faced overboard, landing boozy, bird-glass-bleeding feetfirst into a shiver of fifty frenzied sharks (adios, amiga).

By the time Bob and Fischel were entering the San Diego har-

---

31   a single-man submarine capable of diving to depths of 2,001 feet

bor cruising amid the pedal-boaters of Balboa Park, they'd been tracked and tagged for a grilling. They were immediately boarded by officials of the United States Coast Guard, taken ashore, and sweated in separate stalls. Each succumbed to a lengthy interrogation.

Bob's passport sat pissing in the hand of DHS agent Coco DeMille. DeMille sat tall in his seat, scanning Bob's passport through thick glasses and cross-referencing data lazily on his laptop. On the wall behind DeMille, a framed poster of DHS self-promotion: a square-jawed handsome white agent underlined with the stolen slogan "Dressed to Kill." But DeMille was a slender man, slightly walleyed. The previous evening's bourbon permeated like hot breath from his skin. Sour. Unpleasant. He began his interrogation.

"I see you were in Baghdad in 2003. What was the nature of that trip?"

"The nature?" Bob asked.

"What was your business there? You some kind of hotbed whore?"

Bob squirmed, then sternly said, "I'm no kind of whore at all. I was answering nature's call . . . sir."

Coco dipped his head to gaze over the top of his glasses, pinning his cross-eyes on this curious creature before him. Was this creature clowning? Mocking?

Reflexively, Bob found his own eyes crossing to keep up in the silent mutation of misunderstanding that had become the metamorphosis of their mutual gaze. He realized his subtlety had not been sensed.

"Oh, I see.Yes," Bob said. "Well, the bombing of the US embassy that summer did bring a lot of attention to the city's infrastructure deficiencies. I work in waste management."

"Waste management?" queried Coco. "And was it waste management you were working on in Cuba that same year?"

Bob coughed. "No, sir. Religious tourism. Sensational city."

Coco looked into a file on his laptop, noting the red flags of an Iranian visa and two subsequent OFAC[32] investigations following earlier travels.

"Tehran 2005?"

"A septic systems leech field symposium," Bob replied.

"Belfast '84, Egypt 2011, Israel, Istanbul, Abadabad, Peshawar, Karachi, Beirut, Damascus, Uruguay, Liberia, Sierra Leone, South Sudan, Moscow, Rwanda . . . What's this one, Macau, 1986?"

"I'd forgotten about that trip but I'm aware I went."

"Chile to Managua to Mexico City 2015?"

"I hoped to see MasayaVolcano erupt. I didn't."

"Let me ask you something, Mr. Honey," said DeMille. "Are you aware . . . REMOTELY AWARE of the status of company kept between you and your friend on that yacht off Cabo San Lucas the day before yesterday?"

"Yes," Bob told him. "We shared an interest in tunnels, boat tacos, and I think he liked tequila warmed by the sun. I will say though, I don't know about you, but I'm not one to often be hurried. He seemed a more energetic person than I am. Or, maybe it was just his patterned shirt. Do you know that the Rwandans

---

32   Office of Foreign Assets Control

are pursuing major mining development with the wonder that its own resources may be a curse coming its way?"

DeMille removed his bottle-glass specks, rubbed his eyes, and noticeably shifted tack.

"Let me try this one more time," said DeMille, hoping his unfocused eyes might lend to a less adulterated interpretation of this fellow Bob Honey before him, and perhaps bolster his own patience. He took a deep inhale, followed by a robust exhale.

"Can you tell me about Tripoli, September 2011?"

"Yes, I had been in Benghazi. An entrepreneurial seminar. In Tripoli, I wanted to take pictures. I never took pictures before much. I thought I might get a picture of big female bodyguards,[33] but I didn't. Everybody was very busy at that time."

DeMille then asked, pointedly, "Tell me about your trips to Syria."

"Actually, there they call it Soo-rya. Jesus mispronounced it too."

The room hung silent. Bob then asked, "Agent DeMille?"

"Yes, Mr. Honey?"

Bob, beginning to struggle with DeMille's dermal halitosis, said, "In candor, can you tell me how long you think it would take to get the barge from San Diego to Catalina Island?"

DeMille looked at Bob, whose expression, less blank than a black hole, seized DeMille with a vex of vertigo. While Bob's areas of travel may have raised red flags, and the dates of travel coincided

---

33   Haris al-Has were the giantess girl-band bodyguards who made up the personal protection detail of Colonel Muammar Gaddafi. (Known by Europeans as "Amazons.")

coincidentally with events of note in those regions, it seemed there was something about Bob's benign character that afforded De-Mille's surrender. Shaking his head, DeMille threw Bob's passport across the table to him and excused him with a blunt "Get out!" As Bob approached the exit, DeMille asked him, "You gonna wait for your friend? He's still in interrogation."

Bob stopped and stared blankly.

DeMille's patience with Bob's blasphemy and incongruity of critical thought had run out.

"Yo, clockface!" DeMille said. "Tick-tock! I asked you a question."

"Tick-tock?" Bob asked.

"Are you going to wait for your friend?" DeMille repeated.

"I think he's everyone's friend and in good hands with you. He'll understand if I go. Spiritual people do," said Bob. With that, he absquatulated.

PART II

It is no measure of health to be well-adjusted to a profoundly sick society.

—J. Krishnamurti

Normalization of commercial compromise had left this medium as one of dominantly irrelevant fantasies adding nothing to the world, and instead providing a perfect storm of merchanteering thespians and image builders now less identifiable as creators of valued product than of products built for significant sales. Their masses of fans as happy as hustled, bustled, and rustled sheep. A country without culture? Nothing more than a shopping mall with a flag? Still, business is branding buoyantly, leaving Bob to yet another bout of that old society-is-sinking sensation.

As Bob contemplates his navel, per the instructions of a book on meditation Annie had purchased for him in a new age store, he chants, "Button-button-button. Belly . . . button." Then he hears the knock at the door. It is Spurley again. When Bob opens the door, Cultier is revealed standing on the stoop posing two Popsicles of the barren broad's brew. Bob's ex-wife's salaciously smiling face is brandished on their wrappers.

"Popsicle?" Spurley asks.

"No thank you," Bob replies.

"Good," says Spurley, with a smile. "More for me. Can I come in, Bob?"

In the living room again, they sit in their appointed positions. As Spurley sloppily slurps at one of the Popsicles, Bob can't help remembering similarly slopping sounds made by the woman who graces its package. Embraced as he is by his couch of comfort, he is feeling considerably creeped.

"So, Bob," Spurley begins. "I've been doing a lot of work."

"Yes." Bob nods. "I see."

"Spoke to a buddy of mine down at the ASPCA. Do you not

STATION TEN

BALLAD OF A BROKEN MAN

Back in the alley of the dog, Bob plies the wind-wrapped page of newspaper from his face, in this and direct daylight's return to his derma, he remembers how the sun and sea air, upon his return from Bolivia to Woodview, had taken a toll on his uncared-for skin. Home from his walk, he studies the foreshadowing of his elder years in the mirror, and he wonders if, at nearly sixty, his already deepening wrinkles might at some point come to accumulate unabsorbed Nivea cream. But it is a fleeting cerebration, since he knows he could simply avoid the usage of cream. He remembers feeling the movement of the sea in his body for days after his Pacific voyage return. Sitting at the edge of his bed in those days, weaving and watching television movies—movies themselves, mostly made from the seasickness of misguided creative endeavor.

have a checkbook, Bob? You should consider caution when mailing cash."

"Caution?" Bob asks.

"Yes, caution is something I'm guessing you and I relate to in different ways."

"Really?"

"Oh, mind. I am by no means suggesting that you are without caution. Do you know what I mean, Bob?"

"No, Spurley. But so far, I rarely have."

"Let's make today the day we change that. Whaddya say, Bob?"

Bob thinks. And thinks more. Then, "Okay, Spurley. I'll try."

"You seem a rather practical man, Bob. Your ex-wife tells me the two of you ended up as perfectly good friends in the aftermath of your marriage."

"Yes," Bob says. "Advertising the adversarial is not good branding."

"Advertising the adversarial?" Spurley asks.

"Well yes. Don't you find that people take opportunities to advertise themselves as being *up* in some way?"

"You're talking about the perception of the high-road, Bob?"

"If that's the phrase," says Bob. "I just have to wonder why people have to talk about certain things at all."

"Well, thinking along those lines, Bob, wouldn't offer a fellow like me much job security."

Bob lets out one of his guttural laughs.

"Here's what I've got so far, Bob," Spurley announces. "I've got a lonely man, perhaps spurned by love, perhaps chronically depressed. He keeps odd hours. Disappears for weeks and sometimes months at a time. Makes no effort to meet or greet neighbors. Has, from what I can tell, virtually no social life at all. Likes his BLTs toasted. Has dabbled, over the years, in several businesses. And not only done quite well with them, but they've taken him around the world. And yet, Bob, you don't appear, to me, worldly at all. How am I doing?"

Bob did not listen as Spurley spoke, his own thoughts stirring. "Spurley . . . have you heard the phrase *democracy dies in darkness?*"

"No, Bob," Spurley answers.

"I wonder," continues Bob, "are we the darkness, Spurley? You perceive me practical, yet, it's you who drive a Prius, and myself a Pontiac . . ."

Spurley's loss for words coincides with the ringtone of the phone in Bob's back pocket.

So I just did me some talking to the sun
And I said I didn't like the way he got things done
Sleeping on the job
Those raindrops are falling on my head, they keep
     Fallin' . . .

Bob takes out his cell phone, and masking the screen from Spurley, sees that Annie had just sent him a photograph of herself. When she did that, her portraits were in diligently unassuming poses. Her expressions, as in the one sent this day, never seemed meant to pander toward Bob having one reaction or another. More as though she'd been caught off guard by the photographer. Curiously, Spurley asks, "Whaddya got there, Bob?"

"I don't want to be Eustace Conway-ed."[34]

"The mountain man?" Spurley asks.

"Yes, that's him," says Bob. "Your scrutiny seems like what it might be to be spied on."

"Spied on?" asks Spurley. "Knife collectors?"

"Yes, that's right, Spurley." Bob begins to state an expressed stress. "Edward Lee Howard was a polygraph flunker who got fucked and fled to Finland. Foul news followed when Aldrich Ames aimed high for such a low-ass guy. The Russkies were rigorous in their ruse. They sent Vitaly Yurchenko to play at being anti-Pinko. Foul news TWO." Bob holds up two fingers. "Oooo! You know what's scary? A person who isn't scared. You know how and why Bob's gonna die?"

Spurley interjects. "You are Bob."

"Correct. With a blowtorch to my genitals and a foreign, or non-foreign, cock in my mouth because my fellow American chickenshits will just stand by, including the few graveside who cry. Peace, love, and understanding never did squat for anyone born un-blind. For anybody born poor with a clever mind or in a poor and violent place of their ancestral disgrace." Suddenly, Bob shifts his tense statement's tenor to one of calm attribution, "I tell you this because I love you. —Simply Georgia, 1658."

"You're confusing me, Bob," Spurley says.

"No, Spurley," Bob replies. "It's you who confuse Aldrich Ames with Robert Ames. Do NOT confuse Aldrich Ames with

---

34   an American naturalist and loner who became a reality show star, leading to his arrest by the US government

Robert Ames.[35] Do not do that. And do not confuse me with
Eustace Conway."

"I'll do all I can to take that onboard, Bob. But, are you equat-
ing an article I might write about you with a reality show?"

"Something like that, Spurley. Are you really writing an article?"
Spurley deflects the question. "You interested in spies, Bob?"

"Me?" Bob asks.

"That's right, Bob. Spies."

"I'm interested sometimes. In eyes. Mostly women's eyes.
That's a bit like spies, I think."

"How do you mean, Bob?" Spurley asks.

"Some of them see us and some of them don't. But, they all
see our sins. Don't you think?"

"I don't know, Bob. What would you consider a sin?"

Bob thinks for a moment. "I think I'm interested in spy craft,
Spurley, but have never been a diligent student of it. And when the
world went satellite and cyber, I didn't. Although I do keep a cell
phone, that's true. Let's say I don't know much about these things
in the same way I know so little about women."

Satellites. Sky's eyes.

---

35   Aldrich Hazen Ames was a longtime CIA case officer who became a mole for
the KGB. He was convicted of espionage in 1994 and is widely (and correctly) regarded as a total shit. Robert Clayton "Bob" Ames (no relation), the
CIA's Near East Director, was killed in the suicide bombing of the American
embassy in Beirut in 1983 and is widely (and correctly) regarded as an exemplary public servant.

Women. Real-time transmissions.
High-resolution.
Revolution.

"Isn't everything, and the burden of scrutiny, moving very fast, Spurley?"

Spurley has never heard Bob string so many words together in a row. But before he can query further, Bob clicks on the television set and turns his attention from Spurley. The news is reporting the shootings of five police officers in Dallas. No deliberation in the deification of police officers offered here, when just the day before it was police officers who shot two civilian black men to death. Judge, jury, and journalists had reflexively pre-convicted them of racial rancor by Ruger in a country rife with rule of law. It occurs to Bob that the media had effectively encouraged the killing of cops with that previous day's reporting meant to buoy its own fraudulent negrocentrism and grandiose liberal enlightenment. Today, they shifted gears.

"What do you think about all that, Bob?" Spurley asks, referring to the television's report. "Do you think the police create the problem?"

With his eyes fixed on the television, Bob says, "I think people create the problem, Spurley. White men are afraid of black men. And I can't speak for black men. I don't really know all the statistics but it does seem that fear is a dangerous thing, and not the unique domain of police officers or black males."

The TV now reports that the perpetrator had been dispatched

by police with C–4 explosive by robotic proxy. Spurley sees that this too seems to worry Bob and asks if that is so. Bob responds, "I worry, Spurley, when cause and effect are underestimated. Once subsumption architecture[36] is introduced to popular culture, well, you know, it's never just one side that picks up the trend, or that has exclusive access to tools. 3D printing lesson rules."

Bob turns abruptly to Spurley. "I don't want to be Eustace Conway with a reality show. I don't have a message to promote, Spurley. I don't want to be 3D printed. You might as well write your *ballad of the broken man* without me." Bob explains further, that while he appreciates Spurley taking an interest in him, and that he has indeed considered Spurley's proposition in this moment of his life and its potential to open social opportunity, still, he's changed his mind.

He asks Spurley to leave once and for all.

"I'm sorry you feel that way, Bob. I've spent a lot of time and effort here. I think I've been patient with you. For some reason, I felt that you were ready. Let me ask you one thing before I go, if I must go. That cherry I left in the glass the last time I saw you . . . did you keep it?"

But Bob has already walked to the door and opened it. Unresponsive to Spurley, he stands silently awaiting the man's exit. When Spurley does exit, Bob closes the front door behind him, locks it, returning to his comfort station center couch. Silly questions of cherries saved served to sever any last impression Bob might have had of Spurley as a serious citizen.

---

36   in robotics, a bottom-up design that begins in simplified tasking, for instance, mobility, and is then built upon evolving to complex dynamics

On the television, ISIS-anti-inflammatories, al-Nusra-diapers for men, al-Shabaab-computer coupling, and Boko Haram-diuretics. CHANNEL CHANGE: Israel, Saudi, sickness, and the systemic degradation of the environment. The planet and humankind are feminine things. Their peril a corporate rape, and climate change just another tale of sexual inequality.

Bob's irrational passion for dispassionate rationality is, for him, irreconcilable. The gap between those things we are told and our limited faculty for interpreting them is obvious in any question of cultural complexity, a Rubik's Cube of historical brainwashing, petty crime, and swine-sugar.

He wonders if any notion of intra-culturalism might be foiled by the science of the brain. Where one population has wired its brain to read from left to right, another may take on the same task right to left, top to bottom, bottom to top. Trying to understand those who are differently wired may prove inherent folly. When viewing a face and its expression, is it not true that the same expression may be made or observed in totally contradictory ways depending on the wiring of any given culture? If the left corner of a mouth raised in one culture expresses friendliness or pleasure, might it express unfriendliness and displeasure in another? Are we truly able to understand each other, or doomed not to? Is culturalism explained by brain science, or foiled by it? Or is love only visible in the art of angels and tomorrow's children?

Bob cannot help but worry himself further with these questions. He looks longingly at the pictures of Annie again. Her splendor of unselfconsciousness. Wanton will. The accelerant enzymes her image infuses in Bob create a chemical cocktail he can only counter with self-preservational condescension. A practice he restricts to the privacy of his own home. The Tannerite[37] target of Annie's charms, he stands and presses play on his CD player. Phil Ochs's voice:

> *Play the chords of love, my friend*
> *Play the chords of pain*
> *But if you want to keep your song*
> *Don't – don't – don't*
> *Don't play the chords of fame*

---

37   a binary explosive commonly sold in outdoor outlets for use as a dynamic
     target triggered by impact of high-velocity rounds

STATION ELEVEN

MEIN DRUMPF

His journey ushered in by an era of urban over-development and social decline, Bob's life story might yield unpleasantries upon any close examination. Though he recognized the onset of punctuated equilibrium and the confluence of Spurley's efforts, he's taken stock, and he will not surrender his anonymity at large. To submit to such an attention-seeking deed at this crossroads would be to trade catharsis for coffin. A fight or flight. With this gauntlet thrown down, it increasingly seems that conventional social connectivity was a much more pragmatic remedy than to allow oneself to be exposed to the masses on a lark. His life's success could be quantified by having remained principally unknown to all he'd encountered. His failure, same-same. Bob had run from recognition, recognizing that with it came reputation. Reputation—that infinitely most attackable heel of Achilles. Without reputation, only one's body volunteered vulnerability to viciousness. Only one's body. Bob's, just a blub. Cells, tissues, bioelectrical energy. A blip, barren of the big idea. But now the jig was up. Nothing less than Lima-Charlie[38] to Bob. It was no longer enough,

to just

do

stuff.

This realization created enormous challenges for Bob. In Princeton psychology professor Julian Jaynes's 1976 publication *The Origin of Consciousness in the Breakdown of the Bicameral Mind*, Jaynes suggests that primitive man was not a creature of consciousness, but rather acted in direct accordance to the voice of God. *Heard God Speak!* As consciousness evolved through the ages, so did conflict. There are some historical examples of those theories artifactually—Joan of Arc would be one. Religious extremism, another. Even those behaviors on the spectrum today associated with schizophrenia can be tied to the shaman-esque figures of another epoch. Bob was no shaman. Never heard the voice of God. But man, that Annie can get into his head something good.

Are you in crisis, Bob-beam?

Isn't the whole world, Annie?

Bob sits himself center couch, flicks on the TV. Another debate over guns. Bob sometimes doesn't know what the fuss is all about. It seems to him that words are as lethal as any weapon. Words, unburdened by background checks and available at all times to all persons. Still, Bob understands that assault by word is most typically

---

38   loud and clear

employed as weaponry of domestic dispute and antidemocratic dog whistle. Situations where media interest is minimal, lacking as they do the entertainment value of a warm gun. If society and the media choose to posture themselves culturally as counter to killing, some commonsense control over guns might conform. Still, he isn't sure this yearning for reform or "good news" stories is genuine. It could be said that the public yearning once bent on *belief reinforcement* has now become an insatiable hunger bent on having one's own *insecurity empowered*. It's an exponentially logarithmic madness in the making. In fact, Bob's argument be made, what the cumulative actions and culture of America now yearn for are lawless days and lonely nights for all. A hybrid of race war and civil war amid a massive movement by a plethora of gangs and militias to upset a fraudulent order, posed and imposed by a wealthy few and their conveniently unwitting *puppets for profit*. Problem.

While the privileged patronize this pickle as epithet to the epigenetic inequality of equals, Bob smells a cyber-assisted assault emboldened by right-brain Hollywood narcissists. They of self-righteous hypocrisy, who will give aid and comfort at the bad guy's bidding. Find a gangster galvanizing sales, and you'll find a spokesmodel begging to sell-sell-sell. Find a singular issue of distraction and they and their news hours will dwell-dwell-dwell. Criminal crumbs and corresponding celebrity crusts, bound together by dough. Together they make a mockery of mockery mimicking mystery, and this Bob surmises is the only reasonable explanation for the bloated blond high priest and pavonine of branding. The masturbatory populist who's become a media sensation, and then some, during his candidacy for King, making despots sing. And helping the retro-party, so inviting of the stupid, to conscript the even stupider.

Bob likes Jupiter.

It had been a cosmos full of communist cosmonauts over Indochina that had once frightened boy-Bob in a dream. Ever since, he'd looked to Jupiter for high ground.

But back on earth, Bob likes Woodview, California. He likes California enough that when media maligns it, he makes mental arguments against their methodology. In a red culture that celebrates itself for the origin of farming and other symbols of Americana, they are naive to the fact that California not only supplies 60 percent of all produce domestically, but also is the state that produced both McDonald's and the Hells Angels. If there were a one-only territorial claim for the abundancy of American archetypes, from rural heroism to outlaw ideology to just downright and dogged hardworking men and women in all the United States, it would certainly be owned by California. How dare any marginalize the long Golden State? Damn them to their dopey demagoguery and its devilishness, Bob thinks.

Do you think it's possible to sell your soul to Satan? To a darkness, Bob-beam?

A darkness, Annie?

Yeah, like Led Zeppelin. Didn't they, my gruff goat?

Bob flicks the channel. A young pop star is selling acne medication.

It's manufacturing, Annie. Dark things are manufactured. They're not endemic. We don't give ourselves to dark things. We create them.

Are you creating dark things, gruff Bob-beam?

Bob's head begins to throb. If only he were nine, picking into a rock wall, chipping out artifacts of ten-thousand-year-old sea life. Turritella shell structures, mussels, and Xyne Grex fish. Or maybe riding his red Schwinn raining fire on rivers, riding work-runs with Cowboy, and relishing with regret the chocolate-brown legs of the black girl called a whore he'd never had opportunity to love or explore. Like the heart, brain, liver, or kidneys, skin too is a vital organ. That we are shamed for our love of skin is a bias toward brain minus organic kin. That Bob was born to explore makes neither he nor teenage black chick "whore." He could've been an astronaut, he thinks.

What about space, the cosmos, Bob-beam?

I want to go to Jupiter, Annie.

Jupiter, Gruff? The planet of polar cyclones?

Jupiter. Stupider. Stupider. Stupider. I'm . . .

It's not stupid, Bob. You're not stupid. But you don't have to go five hundred and eighty-eight million kilometers from earth. Think practically . . . just for a second.

Annie does have a way with Bob's brain. Instead he dreams of going to Jupiter, where there was little if any chance of social connectivity, he finds himself balancing on the edge of heartness and sets his mind on hosting an afternoon-social for the residents of Sweet Dog Lane. He'll call a rental company, get tables, picnic chairs, and sun umbrellas, and set the stage on his front lawn.

He sits up evenings individualizing invitations in the form of cute collages. With his X-Acto knife and cuticle scissors, he cuts into photo and art books, tailoring each collage to his best estimate of the personalities of his guests-to-be, drawn from perceptions founded in the face of their homes. He then picks the right afternoon, puts the date and time of the social on the collaged invitations, and walks mailbox to mailbox inserting accordingly.

It is Saturday and sunny. Bob sets up the briquette grill for burgers and dogs, makes a hundred juice-lemon-style deviled eggs, and has soda and beer in coolers. With the first round of meat on the grill, he sits at a center picnic chair on the lawn, collectedly awaiting the arrival of his neighbors. He had set 1 p.m. as his start time. The first to arrive are prompt to the minute. It is a young man and woman of seemingly late adolescence though pushing an infant in a stroller before them. Think Sid and Nancy. Think bruised veins. Think toxic pale skin. Think body odor marching fore from meters away. Bob takes in their approach, calculates their address as a back house to one of the actual invitees' homes. "Are you Bob?" asks the young male. "I mean, dude, are you Mr. Honey?"

Bob weighs his options as the girl picks her nose. He moves quietly to the stroller's edge, peeks in, and checks the infant for a pulse. It takes a moment, but so far these two young cadavers have indeed kept their baby alive. "What can I do for you?" asks Bob.

The young man and woman overlap each other while beginning to answer.

"We—" "We—"

(again)

"We—" "We—"

(and again)

"We—" "We—"

Bob interjects helpfully, "Let's try one at a time."

The couple offer each other looks of deadened deference and then spontaneously shake their fists in a game of rock-paper-scissors. Bob breathes deeply and once again checks the pulse of the infant. The girl's scissors dominate the boy's flattened paper palm.

"We got your collage," she says as her nose begins to bleed. "And, like, we want to pay our respects."

"Your respects?" Bob asks.

"Yeah, to the lady."

"The lady?" Bob inquires.

"Yeah," says the girl. "We like wanna go, but I think it would, like, be all depressing for them," indicating the stroller.

"Them?" Bob asks.

"The twins," responds the girl.

Bob rechecks the stroller, gently pressing around the swaddle of the infant. "This is one child," Bob says.

"Huh?" burps out the young man.

"One child. This is one child. This is not two children," Bob repeats.

The couple again offer each other deadened looks. "Uh-oh," they say. The young man continues to Bob, "Okay. Like that's kind of weird and sort of fucked up, but like . . . if we kind of find the other one, are you cool baby-sitting?"

"This is a community-building exercise," says Bob. "A block party. I am not a child-nurturing individual."

After several beats of mutually confused silence, and the girl's nasal hemorrhage now streaming, the couple depart without comment. They turn the stroller back toward the street and lazily move

back in the direction of whatever cave they'd left. Bob sits back in
his lawn chair watching them aimlessly stroll out of sight. He stays
there, in that chair, still as a statue for nearly half an hour until he
hears the distant approach of circus music just as the first of forty
black limousines cruises past his house. Windows rolled down, his
neighbors cast contemptuous glances upon Bob as they glide by.
As he watches them pass, his eyes drift to a bevy of floral garlands
piled four feet high on the burned-out skeleton of Helen Mayo's
house. It has taken months to certify her death, her scorched body
parts so interchangeably intertwined and intermingled with the
manglement of the pilot seat's turbaned tenant. Bob had inadvertently invited a neighborhood of strangers on the day their pre-
commitment to Helen Mayo's funeral procession prevailed. Only
Bob (and, evidently, one of two newborn twins) had not been
invited. At the back of the line of limos, his ex-wife in her ice
cream truck, randomly reconfirming her self-righteous rebellion.
No sooner do they all appear than they vanish into the hills, the
ice cream music trailing distantly with them. All consideration of
convivial company is quashed. Bob eats a deviled egg and sits till
sunset.

It's a start, Bob-beam. You gave it a go.
I gave it a go.

With night's descent, a galaxy of stars are stripped of their
cover. And to the resident of 1528 Sweet Dog Lane returns a noc-

turnal native knowledge. In the night's finale, as with life's curtain call, there is just no such a thing as posthumous penance. He stands from his picnic chair and lumbers over to the Pontiac, opens the door, sits in the driver's seat, turns on the car, and presses play on the CD player. Phil Ochs's voice:

There's no place in this world
Where I'll belong when I'm gone
And I won't know the right from the wrong
When I'm gone
And you won't find me
Singin' on this song when I'm gone
So I guess I'll have to do it
While I'm here

STATION TWELVE

HARKING BACK: DRIFTING AND DECOMPOSED

In Bob's *saudade*, his memory multiplies moments of longing and dreams. Sharpness of image and sound. If he is to hunt social connectivity, he will have to begin by retracing the wires of his brain and reawakening his lucidity of perception. In 2005, after executing a contract in the Ascension Parish of Louisiana, Hurricane Katrina blasted the brackish inlets, infrastructure, and population alike. With the airport closed due to weather, and later to erroneous reports of civilian sniping, Bob took up in a local YMCA that the American Red Cross hosted for shelter. Of the 150 cots set up on the indoor basketball court, Bob was assigned cot 21-LEFT.

As he dropped duffel from shoulder onto the cot, a drunk young female volunteer, lipstick smeared on her teeth, caught his eye where she sat on the adjacent cot. Her glassy eyes staring up at him. She lifted her red plastic cup toward him, the last of her lipstick sloppily kissed onto its white inner rim. The liquid inside, a pungent iceless blend of available alcohols and electrolytes. In slurred speech she offered, "Put this in your mouth. Smell it." Bob didn't mind drink, but he detested drunkenness. He thought to expedite her aging process, peg her a pensioner, and give her one quick pop on the noggin. He contained himself and left her raised goblet in the lurch. The hurricane's winds felled cell towers, but Bob had thought ahead and brought a SAT phone. As he lay his head down listening to the whirling winds outside, he tried to place a call to HQ. But even the SAT phone didn't want to break through the storm. A-B-C / C-B-A . . . A-B-C / C-B-A . . . And off to sleep he went.

By daybreak, word of the massive flooding and frenzy was building, but the skies had calmed and Bob was able to get through to HQ. Down in New Orleans, within the city center's storm surge carnage, cut-offs, and curfews, a large nursing home had reportedly been remiss to rescuers. Bob sensed an emerging opportunity. Given the force of the storm, and the number of organic projectiles at its peak, there would be ample cover to claim concussive injuries. Bob was deployed. He joined a group of humanitarian volunteers, putting in their boat from a de facto Garden District launch. The day, warm and calm. The water, warm and black. Everything quite still. The only air moving above the city were the pockets rotor-washed by coast guard rescue helicopters. Bob, his mallet holstered, informed the volunteers that there might be a number of elderly holed up in a nursing home in the flooded CBD.[39] The sailors set sail past bloated floaters, ballooned by the bacteria of gut-released gases under too much sun. All facedown and spread-eagle body blimps in the calm black water.

Upon making entrance into the semi-submerged nursing home, Bob and a few of the volunteers found themselves in utter darkness and the waist-deep black water within. In each of their breaths, suspicions of airborne spores. The windows of the several-storied building had been boarded up in preparation for Katrina's fury. With the volunteers dispatching to the highest floor intending to work their way down, Bob remained one up from the entry floor and found himself with the requisite privacy. One hand on a moonbeam,[40] the other on his surreptitiously holstered mallet, Bob kicked in the doors of several residential cubicles on floor two. But with no oldies in sight, he sensed it was a losing game. Usually, when a location has been cleared or evacuated from a hurricane flood zone, the first rescue team on-site would indicate it with a spray-painted "X" on the building's white side.[41] Not so, this nursing home. Nonetheless, a bust. He dreaded the inevitable after-action report.

Surrendering, Bob went back to the boat sensing that the volunteers had at least two additional floors to search. He could be long gone before they noticed. With no obligation to valor, he yanked the rope pull of the outboard, abandoning his fellow

---

39   Central Business District
40   Maglite/flashlight
41   Identification of assault side, specifically in the targeting or navigation of buildings for clarity of COMMS

searchers, taking a slow serene cruise back toward the Garden District on the newfound calm, black sea now flooding the streets of New Orleans town at twilight. In the distance some blocks away, he saw a random house fire. Here, the image of its burn surrounded by water, and the glassy reaching reflection of fire, conjured in Bob a reminiscence of those Molotov cocktails enflaming the river of his youth. It gave an almost surreal quality to his journey, or a flashback to Disneyland's Pirates of the Caribbean ride. A water moccasined serpent slithered by on the surface beside the boat, more bodies bloated by the gases of a bacterial rave, and something in all of this alchemy brought Bob a cathartic sense of momentarily connected bliss; the kind he might, in a pinch, one day pick from his back pocket, were he ever in the greater Gulf Coast area again, and in need of sensory soothing. This brief flirtation with a lightness of being made the velvet voice return to his ear.

"Stop, hey, what's that sound . . . ? Can you hear me softly singing, Bob-beam? Considering killing the elderly in a disaster zone? Don't you fear the devil, beautiful Bob-beam?"

And with that, Bob suddenly saw himself among those full of rage against their own insignificance and subject to the seductions of vainglorious gestalt. The subsiding floodwaters were beginning to expose cells of sanctimony and their cancerous, divisive detriment deluged by adenosine triphosphate[42] delivering de-evolution. It should be noted that New Orleans's famous *Goat of Algiers* did survive the flood.

Oh boy, Bob.

---

42   metabolizes the division of cells

Filthy floodwater drenched, Bob waded his way into the Lafayette Hotel and checked in for a shower. Later, butt-naked and cleansed, he changed the station on a bedside radio that room-cleaners had left on for ambiance. As he turned the dial across Southern stations, he landed on the opening notes of Evelyn "Champagne" King's "Shame." Finding himself reflected in the full-size mirror on the open bathroom door, Bob began to dance. His movement at first slow and behind the beat. But as the music and its pulse rose, Bob began to follow, finally finding the spastic gesticulations that would purge his pond of pirates.

Oh boy, indeed, Bob.

INTERLUDE

TRANSCRIPT

SHERIFF'S BLOTTER – WOODVIEW COUNTY, CALIFORNIA
JULY 17, 2016

"911. What's your emergency?"

"I've got my twenty-twenties on him right now—as we speak!"

"May I have your name, ma'am?"

"Oh, for goodness' sake, I'm so very sorry. I am the daughter of Mrs. Helen Mayo. You know, the lady who just passed. I'm standing on a scissor-lift here at the demo site of my dear mother's home. I've got this scissor-lift at full vertical extension and I can see right down into that terrible man's backyard . . ."

"Your name, ma'am?"

"Oh, forgive me. I am Helen Mayo Junior."

"Helen Mayo Junior, ma'am?"

"Yes, that's correct. Now listen to what I have to tell you . . ."

"You did say Helen Mayo Junior, yes?"

"Yes, I told you that. That's correct. I'm Helen Mayo Junior. But listen please. The lift is a bit wobbly. He's out there in that yard of his pruning a mela-leuca tree in all this wind with his belly out and sweating in his skivvies. I think he's somehow sending signals. I know he's a white man, but sometimes he just looks very Chinese to me. Those awful eyes of his swell with bad deeds, and I don't believe this Chink is just bonsai gardening, if you know what I mean."

"Ma'am, bonsai gardeners are Japanese. Not Chinese. I don't know what signals you think he's sending, but I want to suggest to you that you come down off that scissor-lift. I would hate to hear that you'd been cited as a Peep-ing Tom, and it's a bit gusty out there today . . ."

"Oh my goodness! Oh my goodness . . ."

"Ma'am? . . . Ma'am? . . . Ma'am?"

[*UNINTELLIGIBLE SCREAMING*]

Complainant had fallen and phone went dead. So did she.

STATION THIRTEEN

OPIATES & INCEST

Miami had long been considered a ZTC[43] for activities of intervention by Scottsdale Program operatives. But with the western desert community's contract termination having transferred command and control away from Loodstar and his New Guinean team, Loodstar had seemingly gone rogue and set up independent operations. Financing unknown. Through the network of operators, Loodstar's rumored activities had come to Bob's attention. Cell-phone locators and FLIR[44] drones had been mobilized, mapping the movements of retirees in the greater South Beach area. While there were plenty of international contracts available, Loodstar had always had a great social appetite for the fraternity of

---

43   zone too conspicuous
44   forward-looking infrared

American operators. That, and the cost-prohibitive nature of flying operators abroad, may have encouraged Loodstar to localize his AO[45] to Miami, where he could recruit INCONUS.[46] Best practices would dictate approvals and appropriations from USG when operating INCONUS, but despite rumors of Loodstar's *off the reservation* racketeering, it wouldn't be the going politic to deport a man in grass skirt without having hard evidence of espionage. Still, a suspicious uptick in the premature passing of senior snowbirds in Florida had caught the attention of some in local law enforcement, including some of those who might frown on any covert *company's* culling activities conducted against their senior constituency.

Loodstar's alleged activities are also concerning to Bob. The flamboyant crew chief, fascinated by narcotics, had proven himself loose of tongue. Bob feared exposure should Loodstar be apprehended. It was, in fact, this unsavory aspect of Loodstar's character that had lost him command and control of the Scottsdale Program several years earlier. While Bob and he have never met face-to-face, Bob has to assume Loodstar has his number.

It never occurred to Bob to specifically ask Spurley Cultier which publication he worked for. It rarely occurs to Bob to ask anyone other than himself anything. But now, he has come to a conscious articulation of assumptions around Spurley. Linkage, he thinks, and decides he should pay Loodstar a visit to confirm or clear the connection considered. He enters his bathroom and sits before the marble in consultation. He needs a directive. While

---

45   Area of Operations
46   Inside the Continental United States

finding the odd face of wisdom or fury before him, the mining of marble's dynamic disclosures mandate meditative capitulation of consciousness.

On this day is that capitulation a reach for Bob. Beset by thoughts of Annie, he is monkey-minded. In addition, he registers this day's lighting as being lackluster to the symphonies of stone and structure. He wanders back to the bedroom, sits on the edge of the bed, and clicks on the television, where the blond buffoon aligns himself with Law and Order like a cartoon. It' gets Bob thinking. Could this high priest of branding himself be conspiring *against* the beheading of the unbranded? Could this translate to the preservation of that one-armed banditry[47] that served the candidate's casino's clasp of cash? Was he or Loodstar playing both sides or being played? Has Spurley been a phalanx proxy of duel four-barrel reconnaissance? As he waded into his wisdom's windage, it was all beginning to make mechanized sense to Bob. The candidate's own *Night of the Long Knives*[48] might be on a-*putsch*, or rather, approach, as he himself famously had residences and golf courses in the greater Miami area. All roads lead to Loodstar.

Bob weighs his options. He can drive the Pontiac from Woodview to South Beach in four days, five if he stops in New Orleans. Or he can jump a plane and be there in a matter of hours. His resistance to flight, an avoidance of any sense memory that Annie's last departure may conjure, tips the scales. He decides to put Pontiac to pavement and pick his back-pocket keepsake of connection

---

47 elderly usage of slot machines

48 The Night of the Long Knives, a series of executions ordered by Hitler in 1934 to consolidate his absolute hold on power in Nazi Germany

collected from that prior Big Easy bliss. Before departing, he packs all the essentials from lies to disguise. Then, in his shed, hangs a hook-light and nails a board to a post, painting a prostration persuading message of provocation:

UDAY AND QUSAY POACHED PRECIOUS
PROTECTED PANTHERS FOR PRURIENT
PARTY PICTURES

He takes a post-hole digger to his front yard, where he situates the sign. Finally, he secures the penetralia of his Woodview province with a room-to-room and around the house intertwine of mother-in-law's clothesline.[49] Bob is rarin' road trip ready!

The America Bob drives, from Woodview to New Orleans, is not that one of lore. Not the one he'd known in his earliest cross-continental automotive excursions. Not the one of "pay later" gas stations, vintage diners, and two-lane roads. Only the trains remain in tribute to that spirit refuge now vanquished by modernity's craven trumpery.[50] Vanquished as if by lightning, blinding burdensome myths, and dispersing misbehaviors exposed.

---

49 Mother-in-law's clothesline: a colloquialism for pentaerythritol tetranitrate
    (PETN)–infused detonation cord, which explodes at a rate of 6,400 m/s, and
    resembles common clothesline
50 Trumpery derives from the Middle English "*trumpery*" and ultimately from the
    Middle French, "*tromper*," meaning "to deceive." Trumpery first appeared in
    English in the mid-fifteenth century with the meanings "deceit or fraud" or
    "worthless nonsense!"

Perhaps a truth worth grabbing and holding on to for dear life, that where life is really lived is in simple places of love and happiness. Bob owned neither. And in lieu of that, only solitude would suffice. There are few remaining romantic vistas experienced in the seclusion of reclusive roadways. In their place, interstates, strip malls, retail emporiums, traffic, roadwork, and bottlenecks.

America, it seems to Bob, is no longer that beautiful girl who'd birthed him. But instead, the ghost of a girl he'd never known.

Driving at night through the intermittent expanses can Bob sometimes see the distant amber lights of isolated compounds. Perhaps prisons. Perhaps casinos. In either case, somebody's in there losin'.

It seems many of the towns are built either on the back of vo-techs or on the job security offered by various states' corrections departments. These are just one observer's thoughts from within a white Pontiac drifting through the American nightscape.

Come morning's light, the new day's Bob feels briefly bright, until traffic, like Tinder, takes its toll in travesty upon trails once left fated to foreplay and fairy tale. Bob passes a feature film fourplex and formerly divine deco drive-in. He realizes that not only in road-roaming reality has romance been relinquished to ruins, but the cinemas themselves have been caged and quartered into quixotic concrete calamities of corporatized cultural capitulation. Perusing the menu during a diner stop in San Antonio, Bob is intrigued by the Venison Wellington, a selection that comes with the written disclaimer: "Even though greatest care has been taken, due to the nature of the product, there is a very small risk of bullet fragments that could be found in the meat." Bob decides on a grilled cheese sandwich and is served where he sits by a skinny, vanilla-perfumed waitress. His head hangs over the counter in a meditative first bite. His incisors make surgical entry, initiating a delicately inconspicuous cut through the toasted buttery carapace. His tongue laps the melted cheese as his jaws' pressure squeezes it into his mouth. All systems watering. Delectable. Frigging magic. Frickin' diner grilled cheese magic. Then BLOP! BLOP! BLOP! Black coffee pours into the cup of the place setting to his right. It whirls, burbles, then settles into stillness with the emerging image of a grinning septuagenarian staring Bob in the eye, now reflecting on the coffee's surface. Eyes locked into the reflection, Bob surmises that the image of his own face is being simultaneously counter-reflected in the coffee-mirror of his newfound neighbor. Without lowering his sandwich, his swallow, slowly and quietly, allows that first bite to drop like a Special Forces paratrooper into his belly. As the two men stare into each other's reflections, through the blur of java steam, the old-timer initiates conversation in intermittent mountain twang.

"At least you don't strike me as one of them hipster herbivores."

"Who are you?" Bob asks the man.

"I'm Pappy Pariah of Kerstetter, Kentucky, son. Pastor to the argot-applied Appalachian Archdiocese. I'm the one tellin' your story and intend'ta continue right after ma' coffee."

"My story?" Bob asks.

"Don't worry about that . . ." replies the man. "That undernourished nymphomaniac over there just poured my coffee hot

and black. But don't tell her I said that. Shhh," the man hushes.
"Let me tell ya sumtin':
It takes very little time
to drink a cup of wine
or to destroy a village.
One day soon
it will take a week to conquer the world
and a couple of days to establish a motive.
It currently takes about one hour
to underestimate the compassion
of a stranger,
their face reflected on a burnish of
black coffee in a quaint café.
And, no man learns to cycle rounds
on a paper route especially when he has
egg on his face."

Finally lowering his sandwich, Bob instinctively wipes his mouth with a napkin, inventories the napkin. No egg. But, how could there be when eating a grilled cheese sandwich?

With aleatory artlessness Bob asks the Appalachian, "What's with all the opiates and incest in your area?"

He watches the old man's grin go grim turning from the reflected image to Bob's physical face beside him. Bob returns the favor. The old man steps up, putting his face very close to Bob's. "Could you repeat that question, son?"

Bob does. "What's with all the opiates and incest in your area?"
The man smiles, sits back down, sips his coffee, and answers,
"Just folks getting by."

And so it was . . .

Bob finishes his grilled cheese sandwich, last French fry, and
final gulp of Pepsi with the bulk of its remaining crushed ice.
As he places Pepsi drained genuine Georgia-green Coca-Cola
tumbler on counter, the old man takes hold of Bob's paw with
purchase.

"I see you got that Pontiac out there bent toward the east," he
tells Bob. "The east can get sticky this time'a year. If I were you, I'd
head back west to Scottsdale—if you know what I mean . . ." Bob
glances at the old man's hand, gripped around his own.

"I'll take my chances," Bob says.

"Oh boy, Bob." The old man shakes his head and releases his
grip on Bob. "Son, you gonna do what you gonna do. Just don't
get yourself bit by one'a them Zika mossies. Could compromise
ya bringin' a healthy baby to term."

"I'm a man," Bob reminds the adroit au courant. "I'm not a
girl."

"Yeah?" says the old-timer. "Whatever gives ya comfort."

A bit stymied, Bob asks, "How did you know my name?"

"I wrote you."

"A letter?"

"If that would give you comfort, I'm willing. But, for now,
your home's a tome."

Unsatisfied, but on a clock, Bob pays out for himself and for the seventy-something soothsayer, then forges east, pointing the Pontiac to the parish state and Pontchartrain.

New Orleans is his one sleepover stop en route to Miami and mission. Rest is a weapon. He finds a flophouse on Lafayette Street. After taking his turn at the hall-end common shower where he washes road from body, he goes walking. Following the sound of the French Quarter, he drifts into a bar/resto for calamari and an adult beverage. On the TV above the bar is a live broadcast of the Red-Robed Cleveland King-Making Convention. Bob is interested in hearing what the delegate from Guam might have to say. But between the verbosity of a former New York mayor boasting anti-crime and domestic Brexit bluster and the chatter amongst bar barons, Guam is not to be heard. Nonetheless, the visual effect of their floral shirts and leis offers something less conventional for the convention. That's when the millennials put Bob in their reticle.

Three blocks from where Bob sits with his plate of fried calamari is a club called Checkpoint Charlie's, the hub for acid-dropping youth. Two of its trippers had gone walking and perceived Bob through the glass as a sideways-sitting sphinx with a candelabra in its mouth. Within twenty minutes, Bob's drink has been dosed with seven hits of liquid acid. Within an hour of that, images once reserved for marble manifest ubiquitously. Bob's world alters aggressively. As the blood flow to the control centers of his brain is reduced, connectivity is enhanced in lysergic hallucinations. Conversations between two cultures, between two languages that rarely exist in the same house, are now in their proximity lucid and active. Parts of the brain that hadn't known each other before are put in the same room. The visual cortex plays mediator to quarks, while neuronal networks part ways and sleep in default. In this vortex from subatomic and molecular mitosis, Bob finds a connectedness in New Orleans . . . just not the one he'd planned for. That one he'd hoped to pull as bliss from his back pocket. Nonetheless, Bob adapts as he always does. After thirty-five hours' dancing between expanding flowers, grab-ass gypsies, bingo parlor bivouacs, and images of the people purging payloads of an SU-22,[51] Bob wakes from a final lycanthropic slumber to find himself a day and a half behind schedule. Pontiac to pavement, he sets his sights on Miami.

As the Pontiac's radio reports two-day-old news from Cleveland—the candidate's mail-order bride's plagiarized speech, black militias open-carry AK-47s, and the blond one thinks it neato to leave NATO in the lurch—Bob muses on the likelihood that a new norm may visit America. Random car bombings, claimed erroneously or not, with conceit, provocations, or patronage to Middle Eastern manifestos manufactured in Saudi madrassas. Lone, lonely loonies lacking love beyond their guns. You can't depress the depressed, for whom fear is the folly of static scoundrelism. Never static nor separated from depression, Bob is implicitly immune. He arrives in Miami late the following afternoon.

He goes big and checks in to the Fontainebleau Hotel. Thirteen floors up in Room 1406. Bob drops his bag on the bed, flips

---

51   Russian-built fighter-bombers also operated by the Syrian National Army

on the television. 'Tis the final day of the Cleveland King Maker in all its peculiar pageantry. The Mussolini of Mayberry would be fomenting his flock. To Bob, the hypothesis is clear. Between the id and the superego, the sheep had traded a love of their own children for the chance to cry, "Look at me! I'm a pisser on a tree!" Ouch goes the human heart. Out comes the orator's brain-fart, this Jesus of Jonestown, this blind man to Newtown, spits bile aplenty, to bitch us all down. And with Lonesome Rhodes above the crowd, Bob switches the TV off, moves to the window, and opens the blinds to the bikini-cladders, the beach, and the big blue. Somewhere out in that twinkly blue sea are whales being treated brutally. Bob is bothered by brutality toward beasts, has never been a hunter of animals. In fact, he despises hunting and hunters. They and their easy-kill technologies. Their detachment from the kill. From the purpose. From their own primal existence, and their petty thievery enacted against the noble beasts. With one exception: those who hunt wild boar with their own bodies and a dagger. There is pride to be had where the prejudicial is practiced with precision in the trenchant triage of tactile terminations. This came to him via the crucible-forged fact that all humans are themselves animal, and that rifle-ready human hunters of alternate-species prey should best beware the raging ricochet that soon will come their way.

From his back pocket:

Raindrops keep falling on my head
But that doesn't mean my eyes will soon be turning red
Crying's not for me . . .

His phone calls out to him. It is a photo of a woman's forearm with a deep horizontal gash, bleeding profusely. No message
attached except its sender's codename, "Anasyrma,"[52] who, with
some follow-up, Bob sees has also posted the photograph on social
media. Bob would know that arm anywhere. It is Annie's! The slash,
he thinks, shows all the hallmarks of Guinean fanfare. Is it possible
Annie had been nabbed by Loodstar operatives? Has fate forwarded
him to Florida? Is this a warning, a war declaration, or a soap chip?[53]
Has Bob been surveilled? If so, by whom? And, if Loodstar has
Annie . . . for what reason? Through what reticle or rhyme?

While Bob is no creature of panic, the measure of these uncertain-
ties and his consciously palpable paranoia concerning the sudden and
coincidental circumstances calling Annie's well-being into question
prompts in him a primitivism of perspiration. Optimal blood flow
to his extremities shunted, he breathes deeply. In then out. Exhale
extends to excess. Repeat. Again. Repeat. And with oxygen's return
to his outer cortex and frontal lobe comes homeostasis. He disrobes.
Showers have always helped Bob clear his mind and prepare himself
for remedies requiring rigorous focus. Bob showers and towel dries.

From his go-bag, he pulls a black linen suit, businessman shoes,
and a pressed white shirt. He dresses and exits the hotel onto Ocean
Drive. Crowded with tourists, beach comers and goers, shoppers,
bicyclists, and big ostentatious cars . . . there it happened. From
a perpendicular street came the marchers a-many. Not so much
deplorable as the violently immature followers of the violently im-

---

52   ancient Greek goddess of exhibitionism
53   a psychological operations tactic where fake communiqués are intended to
     demoralize combatants

mature seventy-year-old boy-man with money and French vanilla cotton candy hair. They appear Aryan-esque with their "Yellow Lives Matter" banners and all with yellow-blond hair and eyes of Prussian blue. They chant, "Make America More Yellow!" Bob can't help but consider that the doings and don'tings of the day are less a political or cultural crisis than a cataclysmic crisis of the country's mental health. He makes up that it might be measurably mended by mandatory public service. If only every American might have, or have had, one marvelous moment in their young lives as living proof that they matter. Instead, he is reminded of Big Bob Dylan descanting, "The sun isn't yellow. It's chicken." Then—

KA-BOOOOM! FLICKER-FLASH! SHMOKIE DOKIE AND FIRE!

A concussive car bomb blasts, sending shockwaves, blast wind, and pyroplastic-esque fragmentations through a five-hundred-square-meter radius. Bob is thrown backward but uninjured, shy a brief bout of auditory exclusion. After standing back up, dusting himself off, and relaxing his respiration, he surveys the street before him and identifies the unmistakable odor of plastic explosives, sensing Semtex.[54] Semtex has potent personality and punch. Its hexagonal booster-charge-blast fancy, fulminant, and forcefully familiar in Honey history. With RDX,[55] PETN (Bob's go-to det cord) is the second of Semtex's principal segments. He susses this stash as stock made available from the demilitarized erstwhile Czech army caches captured in the concessions of the late 1980s and early '90s.

---

54 a highly malleable explosive, suitable for all your demolition needs
55 organic compound of white solid explosive classified as a nitramide

Peeking through the mass of yellow-blond bloody body parts, material destruction, and *fallback ejecta's*[56] rain re-devouring, he glimpses the blast crater and molten Miami's underground substructure. Now, our American melting pot so hot, it liquefies the plot. Through the obscuring smoke and flame flashes the face of an exotic dark-haired woman exiting a damaged building from across the street. Her eyes briefly lock Bob's until rejuvenated black smoke and red blades of fire re-obliterate the view. Sirens start to fill the air, and their harkening of that ice cream music most wretched suggests his retreat.

Bob makes his way back into the hotel and drifts toward the lobby bar. While chaos dominates the frantic atmospheric foray upon guests, employees, and scrambling police officers seeking to secure the greater crime scene, Bob spies the bar. An oasis. Tending it, a loath-to-be-bothered barman. This is El Greco Hernandez, and his lounge plays as a shadowy and quiet calm to the lobby's brightly lit territory of turmoil. As the doings in Cleveland play on the television above the bar, Bob asks El Greco simply, "Are you serving?" To which El Greco responds, "I'm always serving." It occurs to Bob, El Greco may be a bit of a *football bat.*[57] Bob sits.

He slowly sips some Russian spirits while staring sparingly at himself in the mirror behind the bar. He contemplates his VMOSA,[58] beginning with his immediate situational awareness. First, he has a bomb scene outside his hotel that has clearly created

---

56 that which has been ejected and then falls back to the site of the explosion or near the explosion's epicenter
57 an individual or way of doing things that is particularly odd
58 Vision, Mission, Objectives, Strategies, and Action Plans

disembowelment for some, and a disruption of mood for many, but is confident that CISD[59]-tasked teams will arrive to settle those souls whose day at the beach had gone BOOMingly bust. Secondly, he has El Greco there, more interested in television than in any situational awareness of his own. Thirdly, there is the original problem: that Loodstar may be active and surveilled in a way that could compromise Bob's cover, and may need neutralizing. And finally, there is the added dilemma that Annie might be involved, caught in a cross fire? Or, in any case, bleeding. El Greco switches the bar television channels back and forth between the after-blast coverage in front of the hotel and the party in Cleveland. Bob wracks his brain and seeks his dog's nose for a starting point. It is then that a female voice comes by surprise from the stool beside him. "You're Bob," she says in an Eastern European accent. Bob nods.

"I am Anasyrma." Bob turns. It is the woman he'd spied after the blast. On first impression, hers is a mischievous if not mystical beauty. She looks roughly Annie's age, and the kind another man might take for a lesbo-leaning lunatic. For Bob, she is his date with danger's dark web deity.

"Don't look at me!" Anasyrma instructs, then whispers, "We can't be observed talking to each other." Bob dutifully turns away but only to adjust his observation of her to the mirror's reflection.

Anasyrma does the same, saying, "That's better. You know this is all unsustainable. We are near the end of days, Bob."

Bob nods, as if to a nuisance claim.

"Do you know who I am?" she asks.

---

59   Critical Incident Stress Debriefing

"I think you sent me a picture," Bob says. "Are you responsible for that bomb?"

She responds bluntly, "Don't ask personal questions." Bob shifts in his seat. She continues, "You know the Marble Palace Hotel? The one with the terrible gold gilding? Everything you're looking for is there."

"Are you from . . . Scottsdale?" Bob asks.

Anasyrma begins to giggle. The giggle becomes a laugh. Soon she guffaws herself from stool to floor. She begins to writhe, cackle, and cough out her laughter uncontrollably. Her eyes watering, she nearly poos. Bob spies what might be a dime-sized and expanding moisture blossom from her rear-end-center, signifying perhaps some minimal ass-piss. Bob looks at her rolling and cackling on the floor. She can only hand gesture to remind him not to look at her. Has the cover of their conversation not already been blown?! Nonetheless, he submits and turns back to the mirror, where he finds he now has to rise on his stool to regain a reflective angle that will allow him a visual on the Eastern European picture poster. After several long minutes of her spasmodic guffawing, Anasyrma begins to compose herself, telling Bob,

"I know all about the Scottsdale Program! People tell me everything because people like posts, Bob. I am a poster, and the third satellite of your syzygy." These words sit Bob back down. "You're looking for Loodstar, am I right?" She informs him that Loodstar has left the elderly-elimination business. That he *is* in Miami with his gaggle of Guinean gladiators and local-hire hostile homeboys. He currently contracts for the man she refers to as "you know who." She describes infighting within the man's own organization. They debate the value the worn players of one-armed bandits offer their casinos. One camp believes them booming to the bottom line. The other deems the decrepit and deflationary injurious to the sustainability of such a branding bonanza, boding badly for P&L.

Lamenting Loodstar, she says he's gotten into the sex trade. Human trafficking. And, according to Anasyrma, is himself financed by the aforementioned "you know who." Her sources identified Annie among the most recent sexual slaves snatched as inventory. "She's at the Marble Palace Hotel." To Bob's now skeptical sneer she says, "Like I told you, people tell me everything."

With that, Anasyrma excuses herself, "I happened to bring my bikini. I'm going to go through the back to the beach and get some late sun and post some selfies until the smoke clears."

As her epicene frame do-si-dos downrange, Bob calls after her. "People tell you everything?"

Anasyrma stops slowly in her tracks and turns to him. "Everything, Bob Honey. That's the new order. The new world. Don't you know that?"

"Know what?" he asks.

She smiles, lights a cigarette, and takes a deep drag, then speaks through egressing smoke. "Narcissism's nasty little secret," she teases. "Oh, poor man. You don't know, do you? You think yourself a killer but there's no one left to kill. Identity is life. The world has replaced its identity with electronics. You, old man—if you don't mind me calling you that—are from a generation of SELF-love. Our only self is . . . well . . . selfies. I sense you are a humble man. You don't have the skills to be anything else."

Bob ponders this, visibly dizzied and distressed.

She laughs, then goes out the back with, "Anasyrma always in action!"

Is her *knowing* to be trusted? Or are these, perhaps, the memetic meanderings of a millennial so advanced by the evolution of informational access that it might render her information inexorably uninformative? Still, it is more actionable than any other intel he has at hand.

Bob turns to El Greco, finding his eyes on him. El Greco leans toward Bob over the bar, beckoning Bob closer with an extended finger, and whispers to Bob, "Charlie Mike,[60] my friend. Charlie Mike." Bob suddenly understands. He pays his tab and tip, then moves to exit the bar, trailed by El Greco's salutation, "*Shukran.*" Without turning around, Bob says, "You're welcome."

Mallet secure beneath Bob's jacket, he exits the hotel to the street. With a few notable exceptions—emergency workers, barricades, cadaver dogs, toxicity teams, and overhead media helicopters—South Beach has become a ghost town. Public threat assessments have considered potential additional bombing activity within the city likely, and authorities have encouraged shop owners to close, residents to stay in, and tourists to flood the airport in hopes of flight. Bob serpentines his way through barricades to his line of departure,[61] then sets off through a heavy shopping district, he a nearly lone figure surrounded by signage. Famous faces of models and movie stars, their airbrushed images like unexploded

---

60   military slang for "Continue Mission"
61   starting position for attack on enemy position

ordnances in a minefield of storefront windows. Billboards, both electric and paper. Is it they or the scent of Semtex filling the air? This conundrum represents a problem-set all its own for Bob. Considering it a coefficient of variation,[62] he carries on. As he approaches the grand facade of the Marble Palace, he considers it may be a hardened site.[63] He pauses and peruses it as a patrol car cruises him suspiciously. He nods toward the hotel as if indicating he were a guest returning to his abode. Seemingly satisfied, the patrol car moves on.

The glass and golden door he gently breaches. Less Trojan horse than matter of course. One foot, then the other, steps inside, the Marble Palace foyer high and wide. With every step he registers re-experience: the echo of his shoes on the marble floor, against its walls, gold-gilded halls, and ceiling. In this tomb of odious opulence, he is startled to notice that the hotel stereo system is playing Morricone's "Gabriel's Oboe." The music moves him to his monkey-mind's mea culpa. Bob approaches the concierge desk. There, a slender young black male in suit and tie stands behind the desk, speaking to Bob as he approaches. "Feelin' beddah?" asks the man.

"Beddah?" asks Bob. He takes a last few steps forward, approaching the young man behind the counter with the intention of further questioning this fella's oddly familiar inquiry. As the man himself sits, it is then that Bob sees the bottom of the man's waistcoat lift, exposing the top band of a grass skirt. Bob catapults into

---

62   a measure of variability and volatility relative to the average member of a
     population or data set
63   a structure usually built under rock or concrete, designed to withstand con-
     ventional, nuclear, biological, and chemical attack

combat! The music takes over Bob's mind, and his mastery of the mallet leaves the Loodstar operative on the floor, head cracked open like a coconut split by a tungsten vise. The ballet has begun. Bob flashes on the surveillance camera above the concierge desk. He's been made. Argus-eyed.

No sooner do the first of Loodstar's troops exit the elevator than Bob dispatches them. Between marble, mallet, and mayhem, Bob is most in his element. In these halls of magic stone can Bob read patterns. Its accentuating phantasmagoria of faces, ancient and contemporary, speak to and navigate him. A wizard's cape breezes Bob to the stairwell. A dragon's tail points him to the fourth floor.

Rise on oboe.

Behind the hallway door, he hears their mercenary mumbling. The Guinean grumbling in dispersement of fire-teams. No offense to the dragon, but Bob assumes higher-ups to higher floors as he bounds the staircase, just one more floor to a suddenly opening door, face-to-face, he topples three tribesmen. Weasels down. How many more? He rushes the corridor.

Rise of strings.

Room 331 just to his right.

The choir sings.

With his mallet, Bob Honey pops the lock. It is time to catch his breath, take a moment out of sight, and a little stock. But inside the room, the television is on. A *Duck Dynasty* star speaks conventionally for the artist of con. Pundits report their version, already inured to the preposterous perversion. A singularly immoral inversion. When Bob sees the locked bathroom door, he gives it three inquisitive taps with the mallet, and then one more. A voice from behind the door.

"Dat you, my bruva?"

Bob recognizes a New Guinean twang coloring this ghetto-ized slang. From behind the bathroom door, "Caught me a case of kuru![64] I crackin' a grizz,[65] my bruva. Give me a minute more."

"Who's in there?" Bob asks. "Identify yourself!" Bob contemplates the RUF.[66]

"It's me," says the man behind the door. "Da bruva you used'a work for."

"I did? I worked for you?"

"C'mon, my Winnie-da-Pooh-mutha-fucka-bruva. Your man Loodstar here!" Bob has always assumed a different personality onto Loodstar than that which he now encounters in their collision. But, he knows his former supervisor is not one to be trusted and will have to be teed off the toilet.

"Can you turn the TV up? I've been waiting to hear what my man from *Duck Dynasty* gotta say."

"Where's Annie?" Bob blurts through the door.

"Who's Annie? She Russian? Ain't seen no Annie on the traffic."[67] He goes on. "Let me wipe my butt. We'll hear out the *Duck Dynasty* boy, den I'll get you some girls and drug'es."

---

64 a virus contracted through ingestion of infected human brain matter

65 taking a shit

66 Rules for Use of Force—Domestic military terminology differentiating from its OCONUS counterpart ROE (Rules of Engagement)

67 traffic: classified intelligence stream monitored only by those in government agencies with high security clearance (and sophisticated New Guinean hackers)

Bob finds himself at the end of his rope. He kicks in the door
of the bathroom, Loodstar, sitting on the toilet, grass skirt around
his ankles. Bob has barely made assessment upon entry when
Loodstar's purse-lipped *PFFT!* sends a dart careening through a
three-foot length of bamboo tubing. Bob's eyes cross, observing its
trajectory as the tree-sap poison dart pierces the thickened carti-
lage of his nose. But before Loodstar can re-load, Bob bashes him.
As Loodstar crumples to the floor like a bloody bag of smashed
asshole, Bob pulls the dart from his nose before the poison has
much chance to be absorbed. He drops the dart into the waste bin
beside the fallen tribesman.

Back in the marble corridor, he moves again toward the stairwell, where the faces of time now guide him to the highest floor. It
makes sense to Bob that whoever is in charge of this outfit would
likely have chosen a suite with a roof garden.

The piccolo plays.

Hearing the sounds of assembled tribesmen now seemingly
swarming from all directions, Bob slips out a window from the
stairwell, where he is able to launch himself from sill to fire escape.
He makes a rapid ascent, where he clears the cornice, collapsing
briefly onto the roof garden. Beyond a grinding air-conditioning
unit, Bob sees what appears to be a skylight. He skull-drags his way
toward it. Looking down into the room below, a terrible sight. A
voyeuristic sideman stands by as if managing the campaign waged
by the ghastly freckled back and the golden blond hair of a fat man
pouncing, puckering, and fucking a slender blonde woman. It is
Annie, he thinks. His arm draws back and he crashes the mallet
through the skylight, sending its shattering glass raining down on

the bed below. The girl screams through the choir of marbleized sirens of song. The pummeling man flounces, exposing a glance of the girl's face to Bob. Paradigm shift. It isn't Annie at all. Nonetheless, has he found Loodstar's libertine? Has he stumbled upon the towering titan of treachery?

Bob jumps through the skylight's fractured frame, landing on the crowded bed below. He pops up onto his knees, remembering,

Slow is smooth

Smooth is fast

And bloody is slippery

As he arches back, mallet raised, the man's big blond head swivels to see his attacker, subjecting Bob to a visage, repulsive in repose, then BANG! The echoing report of the sideman's magnum as its wadcutter target-round pierces Bob's head beside the cerebral cortex, its lands and helical grooves settling and embedding in the inoperable real estate of Bob's brain. His body seizes, folding to the floor. Warm blood escaping the perfect circular puncture behind his ear, pooling, cooling, and coagulating like hot Jell-O on the marble deck. Out-of-breath Guineans gain entrée, weapons drawn. The sideman, his face like hell's hooligan, barks at them to move on. The nude girl seeks solace in a wrapped bedsheet, trembling in paralytic panic, pleading for her passport. Before the arrival of paramedics or police, the unscathed blond man and his hooligan are extracted by helicopter from the roof garden, leaving Bob barely breathing in the sky's broken glass.

Was that broken skylight
his last song and worldly sight?

That sun's rays shafting
through gun smoke
in the late afternoon
its filtering focus
and smell of the moon.
From moment to malady
to montage of pain,
he wondered were he really feeling,
or ever would again?
He observed a familiar sensation
in sensing himself alone,
Might next he go to prison,
or die there on his own?
Would his body be poked and prodded
or simply left to rot?
Then his recall brought back
the words of
Egypt's own Sadat:
"I will die, I will die, I will die
knowing death is not my foe
but not one second sooner, sir
than when
my God
says
it's so."

In less an oddity of adjudication than a predictability of political obfuscation and skulduggery, Bob was never charged with a crime. His neuro-cranial injury, while relatively superficial, left a mark on his mind. A mark on his mind. They must be blind. They cannot see what Bob Honey sees.

STATION FOURTEEN

DEBUNKING CAMUS

Rarefied resins liquefied during a life languishing unloved were beginning to create new free radical initiation of polymerization. The chain reaction had Bob heating, cooling, incrassating, and beginning to cure. Newfound catalysts created by catastrophic systems failure.

What for so many years had seemed a loss of memory function, Bob now observed in himself empathetically as editorial wisdom. In the absence of memory will memory have no influence. From repression concealment, the slaughters that had led to his atonement had opened a celestial door. Necessary no more. For the first time would Bob see the culmination of his fifty-six years without regret, finally accepting that he was born this way. Born with a bullet in his head.

A mind is bending, twisting, turning, floating. It inhabits hur-

ricanes, earthquakes, outbreaks, and elections. It contemplates the
rise of locusts. In Bob's morphine dreams at Jackson Memorial, the
desert debunked Camus.

So said the French Algerian:

Truth, like light, blinds.
Falsehood, on the contrary,
is a beautiful twilight that enhances every object.

His dream's desert daylight diffusion dictated disturbances in
the void of visual detail. Rocks not yet sharpened by shadow. Colors washed clear by high sun. Incandescent is as incandescent does,
hence flat light sight for Bobby-boy was no sight at all.

"Button-button-button. Belly button." Bob practiced the Zen
breathing of Annie's book, extending his dream of the desert till
the sunset. Now, Bob thought, could something truer be told.
If you've never flown a single-engine craft in a South Sudanese
sandstorm, put your seat belt on! Drifting into his dream were
donkey-blue diatribes from the next bed's TV. Philadelphia, feelin'
the *burn*. Daytime speeches twist and turn. And celebrities yearn
to be close to those taking an evening stage turn. The Man from
Chicago spoke, drawing an oratory ace from beneath his cloak.
Bob listened, but never woke. The wind and tumbleweed of his
dry desert land whispered a speech from its own parched earth
and sand. Then, the television switched to a German rock band.[68]

---

68   AnnenMayKantereit

Sometimes,
Sometimes I like to lie
I don't know why
I don't know why

In this desert of Bob's dream did disturbances seem a truth of beauty. For the first time did Bob feel himself a thing apart, renewing value as the low light's heart declared the desert hollows a directive.

Sometimes,
Sometimes I fool strangers
I tell them wrong names
I tell them lies
And they're mostly the same
When I tell them about my past
There is nothing that'll last

The horizon's shuttering red skyline drops behind a summit of time.

Sometimes I say the truth
Maybe just because of my youth
Sometimes I like to lie
I don't know why

When an orderly returned to the channel of the lame duck's inspiriting speech, Bob began regaining consciousness. *Felt* this man's words speaking directly to *him*. Hard in this world to be an elegant man, Bob thought, but when his game's on, that Chi-Town-Kenyan-Kansan can-can-can. Then there she was—the woman of our political hour entering stage left. The crowds rise up in glee.

Her opponent might be tweeting, admonishing repugnantly.

As the orderly reduces volume, Bob hears a distant choo-choo whistle.

Just a klick or two from the hospital, cargo containers on rail ride station to station. City acoustics travel trains with doubtless purpose. Sounds of morphine all their own. Sounds that built this country with black and Chinese hands, and the genocide of Indian bands. As the orderly leaves the room, he utters, "Every war we've ever lost has been somebody else's civil war."

Bob sits up in bed, and through the window watches Old Glory waving wistfully in electric illumination atop an adjacent building's spire. He thinks aloud:

"I pledge allegiance to the flag of the United States of America and to the Republic for which it stands, one nation, indivisible, with liberty and justice for all."[69]

Bob lies back on the bed, pulls an iPod from the bed tray, ears-up, and presses play. Phil Ochs's voice:

. . . even treason might be worth a try
This country is too young to die,
I declare the war is over . . .

---

69 The Pledge of Allegiance was written by a socialist in 1892. The version above specifying the United States, in 1923. And not until 1954 were the words "under God" added in response to the Communist threat.

STATION FIFTEEN

JUST A LITTLE KISS

It's August 21, 2017. A driver drives. A sole passenger in bandages sits on the bench seat in the rear of the vehicle. As the automobile hits intermittent speed bumps, its radio reports the accidental gas-line explosion of a Woodview neighborhood home on Sweet Dog Lane. Its only surviving fragment, a posted placard reading, "THE ECLIPSE HAS COME QUICKLY." The report shifts to Midwestern viewings of a solar eclipse unseen in the far west of California. The passenger wonders if the sun might have looked ashamed after being uncovered, like the nightmares of an eight-year-old who's arrived at school unknowingly unclothed to face the laughter of cruel classmates. Was that our new America revealed? Was that the reveal of our humiliated sun intrinsically casting flaming hands to cover the fiery crotch of our country cringing? The vehicle passes under the shade of an old oak and onward to a halt.

Blank-eyed and bandaged head, Bob exits the small white shuttle van, and pays its driver. Grabbing his two suitcases, he moves slowly toward a building of indescribably faded color. A color not unlike those of Irish walls painted in the rain. Above the entryway of this assisted living facility, a branded aging logo of the new billionaire president's name. He walks past wheelchaired VFW members and decrepit oxygen tank breathers. As he approaches the admissions desk, he notices an unusual thing. Sitting atop the desk's counter, an un-potted plant balancing on its rootball. Some kind of Caprifoliaceae. Perhaps a teasel? Appearing from behind the plant's obscuration, a bioluminescently beautiful young woman, the rims of her blue eyes haloing from behind brown contacts. A face so familiar. He must know her from somewhere. Is he blanking a buried memory? Perhaps prosopagnosia? Maybe it is a confusion caused in conflation between the institutional nature of her fitted white shirt and the girl it adorns? Or might it be her garment's microthread-seamed shoulders that throw him? But then comes the gentle velvet voice, "May I help you?"

He pauses and ponders her pleasantry and pout before shyly sharing, "I want to be admitted."

"Well, of course, sugar," she says. "Name?"

He pauses. Then, in cautiously questioning containment, responds.

"Goat. Gruff Goat . . ."

"Let me get you sorted, Mr. Goat," says the beautiful young woman.

After some time in processing, an orientation tour, and the assignment of a residence on the second floor, the beautiful young woman walks Bob to his room. After unlocking the door, she hands him the key.

"This will be your new home."

Bob nods. As he enters his room, consumed of antiseptic air, he begins to close the door, leaving the young woman in the hallway, but her hand halts the door from closing. He offers little resistance. She pushes it open enough to ask him face-to-face, "Are you better now, Bob-beam?"

His face stoic and still as a single silently streaming tear descends over the remaining contour of his condition.

He answers, "I'm better now, Annie." The beautiful girl leans between door and jamb, kissing Bob's teared cheek gently. He finds a hair clip in his pocket and presses it into her palm. They close the door between them and in the corridor, he hears her footsteps patter away into silence, and in that silence does his solipsism sing his eyes dry. Bob finds his bags sitting in front of his bed where an aid had pre-positioned them. He moves to the window of the retirement home and opens the blinds. There in the parking lot he notices an auto on approach—a bangin' black 1985 Buick Grand National. In its time, the fastest US assembly-line car ever built. Zero to sixty and back to zero in a turbocharged ten seconds. At top speed, a Corvette-killing 120-ONE mph car to the Corvette's petty 120. Add nitrous injection to this beastly battering ram and you had yourself the marauder of muscle cars. Behind its wheel, parted from his patronizing Prius . . .

Spurley Cultier.

Spurley stations the Buick in the shade of an oak. Bob had anticipated him an amateur. An anticipation now matured. In the

pro-ranks, there are second-nature checklists. Any sense of height-
ened sensories in a shady hide would be noticed and corrected.
Spurley is, at distance, nearly unrecognizable under the shadow of
the oak. But, what he has clearly not noted is the blade of low-
lying sunlight that illuminates his mouth like a beacon. Does he
not notice its wily warmth? This utter and insensitive lack of pro-
fessionalism and surrender to sophomore spy-craft SOP[70] offends
Bob deeply enough that his strategery begins to huddle around a
play of rarely employed humiliation.

For many in Bob's biz, a pre-operational mantra is practiced
to calm the nerves, steady the hand, and blind the conscience.
With Bob's nearly cosmic ability to read lips did he quietly
chant aloud in perfect harmony with the movement of Spurley's
mouth's mantra.

"Chinese boogie dancers and pale-headed priests, vodka and
tonic, life may be deceased. But I still know what's cookin' in the
oven, and, man, I know the beast."

Do you, Spurley? Bob wonders. We'll see about that.

Who knows what may be that bastard Spurley's weapon of
choice? Likely a g-u-n, spelled p-u-s-s-y. Or maybe a piano wire
garrote, spelled q-u-i-e-t.

Bob considers this briefly, then approaches one of his two suitcases, zips it open. From it he lifts a small Remington typewriter,
carries it to the provided desk. In the drawer of the desk, he finds
retirement home letterhead stationery. He rolls it into the typewriter and begins:

---

70   standard operating procedure

Mr. Landlord,

So, I see you've sent a lackey to finish me off. Perhaps you've underestimated me. Perhaps you've underestimated us all. Our will to face attrition, to die, to kill, to be persecuted, to be shamed and humiliated. Our will to be mocked by your army of sycophantic provocateurial propagandists is eternal, hungry, and inviting. Many wonderful American people in pain and rage elected you. Many Russians did too. Your position is an asterisk accepted as literally as your alternative facts. Though the office will remain real, you never were nor will be. A million women so dwarfed your penis-edency on the streets of Washington and around the world on the day of your piddly inauguration—unprecedented (spelling okay?).

We, not you, own the most powerful weapons on earth—our dreams, the science of physics, seismology, geology, topography, and typhoons. Common sense and a child's experimental taste of dirt, so common to the grown-up boys, girls, colors, creeds and football players you divide. At the bottom of any fissure, a reconnection. We've seen rock walls of time, space and the pace of water. They are not your buildings of bargain. Your gasconade and cache of catchphrases, so limiting and reflexive, escalate the emasculation of you by a world whose patience is in nuclear peril. These sciences and sensibilities are our guns your narcissism neglects. Weapons your NRA masters are incapable of proffering for profit, and outside your dutiful military's might, mandate or mission. So, to your attempt to posthumously assassinate our Founding Fathers, and bait and switch your core, I say I will eat where the fish are glowing. You are not simply a president in need of impeachment, you are a man in need of an intervention. We are not simply a people in need of an intervention, we are a nation in need of an assassin. I am God's squared-away man. I am Bob Honey. That's who I am. Sir, I challenge you to a duel. Tweet me, bitch. I dare you.

A nearly indiscernible smile comes to Bob's face as if for the first time he'd been gently touched by the hand of God and the zephyr breeze of his zenith. He rolls the letter out of the typewriter, folds it meticulously into the size of the small envelope appropriated from the desk drawer, boldly licks the glue strip with his own tongue, and seals the envelope. He then saunters down the stairs to the landing above the foyer. From there, he can observe unseen. First, re-clocking Spurley through the windowed facade, still sitting in the Buick beneath the oak, mouth no longer radiating, but still regrettably conspicuous. Within the foyer, a communal television plays the news. On camera, an anchorwoman, who in Bob's younger days, would've been thought more suited for a guest role on *The Love Boat* than for her current lead role relaying rumors to our republic. Her editorial, in strong opposition to the woman who was the other side's selection. As the anchor satisfies her audience's appetite for absolution. ". . . She was absolutely the worst possible candidate to represent the party."

Really? wonders Bob. As a mind that had managed thought in the silent circumlocution of sentences suddenly sharpens. Not charismatic enough for you folks? Too shrill? Too hawkish? Isn't it true that you never wanted qualifications? You wanted a star, you wanted to be charmed, seduced, and entertained. Was she the worst possible candidate or are you the most arrogant, ill, and unqualified electorate in the history of the Western world? And what does it matter now? She never came to entertain you. Neither did I. You want to kill me because I won't blow you hard enough? You want to kill me because I don't really believe we're the "best" country in the world? Because I don't want to buy a used car from your boss, or don't believe in the gods you lie to? You want to kill me, you boogeymen and women, you worshipers of tits, ass, and beefcake, you sniveling, vomitus, kike-, nigger-, towelhead-, and wetback-hating, faggot-fearing colostomy bags of humanity? You should'a-been-aborted skanks, you want to kill me? You want to kill me? Queue up! And if you don't have a VIP pass, they'll take you for your pussy or your cash. And if you don't have pussy or money enough, then queue up as cattle, behind your bourgeois beasts and traitor-in-chief. You murderers of man and nature. Queue up, you, behind those VIPs you worship in redundancy as they worship themselves with you.

Oh, my beautiful, Bob-beam. I must help you let off steam. There's a place of tenderness that somehow your standards try to, but cannot allow. This is why they hate you. Why your love for me . . . is NOT true. Yet, mine for you exists, without my being by your side. Mine for you exists despite the way you cried and lied. Still, I need you, beautiful Bob-beam. —Yours, Annie. My love and vagina (on your team).

From his position at the landing, he now steps into the foyer and approaches the beautiful girl at the counter as though they'd never had an encounter before. "Would you let me lick . . . a stamp?"

"A stamp?" the girl asks in her adorable accent. "A postage stamp? You mean like for mailbox mail?"

Bob pauses with patience, then, "Yes, a postage stamp, please."

From a drawer behind the counter, the girl produces a roll of stamps, and hands them to Bob. He tears three from the roll, licks each one, enjoying them as if they were grape lollipops, and affixes them to the envelope.

"Please post this for me," Bob says as he hands the girl the envelope and returns the stamp roll.

The girl looks bewildered as she accepts the blank envelope. "But to whom am I posting it? There's no address."

Bob replies, "Post it to the landlord."

Before leaving the counter and the bewildered girl, Bob glances over his shoulder where through the front glass doors he can see that indeed Spurley is still there encamped in his vicious vehicle awaiting opportunity. Bob makes a point of walking a wide banana to the stairs so as to be sure to be observed. He returns to his room, finds his second suitcase, zips it open, and pulls out a hat box, placing it for luck on the bed. He then withdraws a sleeping mask, iPod, and an envelope addressed to the ASPCA with a bundle of cash he shuffle-checks, then seals inside. He lays himself on the bed, pulls the sleeping mask over his eyes, presses the earpieces into his ears, and sets the envelope on his chest. With a delicate touch of the iPod, Phil Ochs sings:

I can see him coming
He's walking down the highway
With his big boots on
And his big thumb out
He wants to get me
He wants to hurt me

He wants to brii-ii-ing
Me down
But sometime later
When I feel a little straighter
I will come across a stranger
Who'll remind me of the danger
And theh-eh-eh-eh-ehhn
I'll run him over
Pretty smart on my part
Find my way home
In the dark.

EPILOGUE

What would be a nightmare?
What would be a dream?
One thousand golden churches?
Melted wings of clotted cream?
Communes of corruption,
in no mood for nuanced things
just tit for tat instructions
as the pompous pendulum swings.
Cyber wars a-wagin'
by hands that seem so clean
while Yemen's children die
in a terror best unseen.
In aggregate atmospherics
our country dance boots
burst its spleen.
Fussy fated fusion fists
at the tip of a laser beam.
From Jupiter it must look so small
the petty pustule bickering of it all—

in war between women and men
un-adhering to nature's call.
At the Mandalay in Vegas,
so much terror death and shock
little men made big
by legal bump fire stock.
Sexual misdoings awakening a rage
Net-pix recasts readers,
hiding its cabal
with the "slick Ted" turn of a page.
Though warrior women
bravely walk the walk,
derivatives of disproportion
draw heinous hypocrites
to their flock.
A child's question comes on Sunday
"What if Monday died?
Would there be only six days a week to live?
And if Monday can die,
so can the rest of days
and I."
Puerto Ricans catching hand towels,
but they have no home nor light
So let's all just be loving
no need to scream and fight.
Fat men tell fat lies
while G-men sift their treasures
this season of treason's triumph

under Moscow's active measures.

There are no men nor women

only movements own the day

until movements morph to mayhem

and militaries chip away

whether North Korean missiles

or marching Tehran's way.

Where did all the laughs go?

Are you out there, Louis C.K.?

Once crucial conversations

kept us on our toes;

was it really in our interest

to trample Charlie Rose?

And what's with this "Me Too"?

This infantilizing term of the day . . .

Is this a toddlers' crusade?

Reducing rape, slut-shaming, and suffrage to reckless child's play?

A platform for accusation impunity?

Due process has lost its sheen?

But, fuck it, what me worry?

I'm a hero,

to Time magazine!

Mandatory service

might humble a man, woman, or three

but it all adds up to a scratch

when "we" is never we.

They'll do all that they can

to scare, play and distract you,

keep you up all night
with news of nothing but a who's-who.
Some seize on scientology,
padlock wives inside a cupboard
So when is it time to say,
"We all knew about Ron Hubbard!"
And while we feuded, failed, and fought,
we watched Sagan's precious dot
turned tawdry on its axis
raising humanity's mortal taxes.
Net neutrality no more,
have we all become the big man's whore?
So rattled, addled and saddled
our entitlement is recklessly embattled.
Hawaiians felt the drill
while denial had thirty-eight minutes to kill,
but the mainland's recognition?
Too exhausted, so quickly left nil.
And Bob? Well, he's been resting
hours have gone by
here's what we must see
when survival tells no lies.
Night has fallen over the retirement home.
The elderly sleep in their beds.
The Buick door creeps open,
amber security lights overhead.
Step by step he approaches,
a killer disguising his dread.

When he crosses foyer to counter
the blonde, face down,
resting her head.
"Excuse me, miss," whispers Spurley.
"I'm looking for a Bob?" he said.
The girl's velvet voice gently answers,
"A man named Bob is doing his job . . . in bed."
But underneath the counter unseen
had the voice really come
thrown so clean
from Annie, completely bald and in underwear
and body so supple and lean.
And the girl seen resting her head?
Gosh, she suddenly looks big
over there.
Her tight shirt of institution
around shoulders bursting
its microthreads bare.
Then suddenly lurching like lightning
charges that blonde-haired body so big
Oh, boy— Oh, boy— Oh, boy—
That blonde girl is Bob in a wig!
Spurley sped for cover
in shield of tendril-rooted teasel
but Bob wields his wild mallet
POPPITY POP!! . . . will drop the weasel.
Spurley concusses like a canvas
its skin splayed from its easel

drops a load in his dewy drawers
spreading a sewery stench of diesel.
No humanity of hows
nor witness to whys
He coughs up his gas bloating guts
bends over desk
and dies.
Cascades of curdling blood
pour past Annie's eyes.
Though she now screams in horror,
so finally complicit is she,
Sounds a bit like us, don't it?
In love and killing . . .
completely complicit
are we!
And Bob Honey?
A being.
Unbranded,
unbridled,
and free.

ACKNOWLEDGMENTS

The author wishes to thank his children for their challenging brains, wit, and sometimes biting wisdom. His comrades in the daily grind of getting printed words to page, Joseph Sacks and Sato Masuzawa. David Blum for his excellent early guidance and Audible advisement. Brilliant Bob Kerstetter for kicking in fifty of this book's best words. Mollie Glick for navigating new waters in publishing, and my many friends whose diversified array of professional experience and expertise has rubbed off just enough to let Pappy play at profundity with the proverbs of their professions and nobility of their nomenclature. Finally, to Peter Borland, my first and best written word editor, for showing me such a smart and supportive process, and never balking at the bizarre. Without the above, this novel would not be. —s.p.

CREDITS AND PERMISSIONS

"Love Me, I'm A Liberal"
Lyrics and Music by Phil Ochs
Copyright © 1965, Renewed 1993, Almo Music Corporation on behalf of
Barricade Music, Inc.
Used by Permission. All Rights Reserved.

"I Kill Therefore I Am"
Lyrics and Music by Phil Ochs
Copyright © 1971, Almo Music Corporation on behalf of Barricade Music, Inc.
Used by Permission. All Rights Reserved.

"When I'm Gone"
Lyrics and Music by Phil Ochs
Copyright © 1963, Renewed 1991, Almo Music Corporation on behalf of
Barricade Music, Inc.
Used by Permission. All Rights Reserved.

"Pretty Smart On My Part"
Lyrics and Music by Phil Ochs
Copyright © 1971, Renewed 1999, Almo Music Corporation on behalf of
Barricade Music, Inc.
Used by Permission. All Rights Reserved.

"Chords Of Fame"
Lyrics and Music by Phil Ochs
Copyright © 1971, Almo Music Corporation on behalf of Barricade Music, Inc.
Used by Permission. All Rights Reserved.

"War Is Over"
Lyrics and Music by Phil Ochs
Copyright © 1968, Almo Music Corporation on behalf of Barricade Music, Inc.
Used by Permission. All Rights Reserved.

ABOUT THE AUTHOR

Sean Penn won the Academy Award for Best Actor for his per-
formances in *Mystic River* and *Milk*, and received Academy
Award nominations as Best Actor for *Dead Man Walking*, *Sweet
and Lowdown*, and *I Am Sam*. He has worked as an actor, writer,
producer, and director on more than one hundred theater and
film productions. His journalism has appeared in the *San Francisco
Chronicle*, *The Nation*, and *The Huffington Post*. This is his first novel.

DISCARD